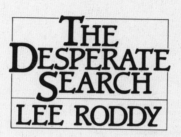

THE DESPERATE SEARCH

LEE RODDY

THE DESPERATE SEARCH

LEE RODDY

BETHANY HOUSE PUBLISHERS
MINNEAPOLIS, MINNESOTA 55438
A Division of Bethany Fellowship, Inc.

Library of Congress Catalog Card Number 88–063476
ISBN 1–55661–027–0

Copyright © 1989
Lee Roddy
All Rights Reserved

Published by Bethany House Publishers
A Division of Bethany Fellowship, Inc.
6820 Auto Club Road, Minneapolis, Minnesota 55438

Printed in the United States of America

For my second grandchild,
Zachary Steven de Haas,
born Oct. 2, 1988,
to my daughter Susan and
her husband, Alfredo de Haas.

AN
AMERICAN ADVENTURE
SERIES

LEE RODDY is a bestselling author and motivational speaker. Many of his more than 50 books, such as *Grizzly Adams, Jesus, The Lincoln Conspiracy*, the *D. J. Dillon Adventure Series*, and the *Ladd Family Adventures* have been bestsellers, television programs, book club selections or have received special recognition. All of his books support traditional moral, spiritual, and family values.

ACKNOWLEDGMENTS

I want to gratefully acknowledge those people who shared their Great Depression memories with me over the years. Their names cannot all be recalled, but their stories will never be forgotten.

I was the oldest of ten children growing up during that period of incredible economic hardship. My recollections are naturally helpful in writing this series. However, the sense of time and place necessary to make these novels "real" is enriched by those who voluntarily shared their experiences with me.

Sometimes it was only a single minor incident that struck a responsive chord in my mind. Sometimes it was a dramatic event or moment, forever frozen in time, that was passed on to me.

So, while all the characters in these novels are fictitious, many dramatized incidents have a historical basis.

A twelve-year-old child did come home to find his destitute family had moved without warning. That was one less mouth for the frantic parents to feed, and they reasoned the child was old enough to take care of himself.

Desperate parents did give away their children to strangers in order that the kids might survive.

Half a century later, I came across their stories and used them as jumping off points for my imagination.

So I would like to acknowledge the contribution such episodes made to these novels. I also want to specifically mention individuals whose Depression memories helped in making those hard times live again in these pages.

Chief among those are my 93-year-old father, T.L. "Jack" Roddy, whose memory is marvelous; and my mother, the late Neva D. (nee Gordon) Roddy. Over the years, she laboriously penned hundreds of notes with the hope they might someday give me "an idea for a story."

The many others who are gratefully acknowledged are Lucille Roddy, Gladys (nee Clewett) Armstrong, Buck and Bea Hudson, Ruth Crisman, Vicki Dunnam, Roger O'Brien, Earl Brannan, Sid Kirsche and Bette Theriot.

For those who are not mentioned here but perhaps should be, I ask forgiveness. Everything I wrote in this series was to try recreating, for the present and future, some sense of what it was really like to have lived through that incredible American Adventure: the Great Depression.

If readers of these novels understand that period and the people of that time a little better, this author's time has been well spent.

To all this I add my fervent prayer, "May it never happen again!"

CONTENTS

Contents

OFF TO A BAD START

As Hildy Corrigan eagerly peered through the windshield, looking for the Mississippi River, the old Essex car coughed, sputtered, and died.

Instantly, all cheerful chatter stopped.

Molly Corrigan, Hildy's stepmother, grabbed baby Joey tightly in her lap, and the six barefooted girls in the backseat crowded forward.

Joe Corrigan guided the silent sedan off the graveled country road onto a brush-covered shoulder.

In the sudden stillness of that late June afternoon, twelve-year-old Hildy disentangled her slender body from four younger tow-headed sisters and leaned over the front seat. "What's the matter, Daddy?" she asked anxiously.

Too busy to answer, her father set the brake with one sturdy, tanned hand while the other flickered rapidly across various knobs on the dashboard.

Elizabeth, Hildy's practical-minded ten-year-old sister, tapped Hildy on the shoulder. "Does that mean we can't make it to California?" she whispered fearfully.

Martha, three years younger, made a disapproving sound. "We're still in Illinois, so 'course we can't make it!"

Ruby Konning, Hildy's Ozark cousin, shook her tomboy-cut blond hair. "We'uns jist got started!" she snapped. "We gotta make it. We jist gotta!"

Hildy didn't say anything but swallowed hard. In these difficult times she had long dreamed of a "forever home," a place where they could all live together happily. But now her dream was slipping away.

Joe Corrigan slammed his hand against the steering wheel. "It's no use! We'll never get there by Saturday morning," he exclaimed. "There goes my job, the house, everything we had waiting for us at Lone River."

Molly shifted the thirteen-month-old baby in her lap and spoke soothingly. "Now, Joe, you're a good mechanic. You can fix whatever's wrong."

"Not in time," he cried, his eyes red with weariness. "I drove day and night from California to get here, and that wore out this old box with wheels. I should've traded it off before starting back to Lone River with all of you."

"Y'all still got seven days," Ruby reminded him in her heavy Ozark accent.

Hildy couldn't bear to lose her dream. Shaking her waist-length brunette braids away from her face, she impulsively reached her slender arm across the backseat and gently touched her father's shoulder. "She's right, Daddy," Hildy said, her blue eyes brightening. "You drove from California to Illinois in five days, and we've got a full week to make it back. Take a day to fix the car. You can do it."

Joe Corrigan slowly shook his head, his weariness etching deep lines in his face. "This wreck can't be fixed."

"Then trade it!" Hildy cried.

"You saw me try to do that already. Nobody wants this cracker box."

"Have you got money to buy another one?" Hildy's eager face snuggled close to her father's stubbly beard.

"Maybe," he admitted, "but this Depression makes it hard to let go of any hard cash."

Hildy shook off her own feelings about how hard times were in 1934. "Can this car get us to Granddad Corrigan's farm?" she asked.

Her father nodded. "If I can get it started, I suppose it could limp there."

The others had slipped into silence as strong-willed Hildy's voice rose with determination. "Then let's do it, please!" she cried, her hopes rising. "We've got to get to California within the week. We've just got to, Daddy."

Her father looked at her with understanding eyes even though he and his oldest daughter were opposites. He always took life as it came, but Hildy made things happen. Slowly he nodded. "I'll take a look under the hood."

There was a collective sigh of relief from all except the baby. He slept now, thumb in mouth, on his stepmother's shoulder. Hildy smiled reassuringly at her family. "We'll find a way," she said softly.

She sounded confident, but inside she knew that everything she dreamed about was in jeopardy.

After a lot of tinkering under the hood, Joe Corrigan finally got the Essex running. Dusk settled over the countryside as the old car eased through the last wire gate before their destination. Carefully, Hildy's father inched across the twelve-by-twelve timbers that served as a bridge over the unnamed creek running through Granddad and Grandma Corrigan's heavily wooded Illinois farm.

Hildy's heart beat faster as she caught a glimpse of the place she hadn't seen in three years. Her grandparents' two-story white house stood on a small hill overlooking the Mississippi. Large, old maple trees filled the spacious front yard. The house needed painting but otherwise was in good shape. Behind it stood the familiar smokehouse, well, cistern, harness shed, silo, outhouse, and barn.

As the Essex made its way up the long driveway, a small flock of slate-colored guinea fowls scattered, crying out sharply in alarm.

Within seconds Hildy's grandparents, both short and stout,

stepped out onto the screened-in side porch. Waving in recognition, they hurried into the yard, past an apple tree, and into the driveway.

"Well, now!" Granddad's white handlebar moustache bobbed above his smiling mouth. "Maude, look who's come to visit."

"I got eyes, Edgar," Grandma Corrigan playfully replied, almost waddling toward the car. "Hello, hello, everybody. Light and sit a spell."

Elizabeth, Martha, Sarah, and three-year-old Iola climbed out of the Essex and ran with glad cries to greet their grandparents.

Hildy held back slightly so her four sisters could get in their hugs and kisses first. She also wanted to stay with her cousin. Hildy sensed that Ruby felt out of place.

Ruby was a year older than Hildy. Her mother was dead, and she had never known her father. Because people had said so many cruel things about her back home, Ruby developed a pugnacious tomboy attitude.

She would fight with words or fists at the slightest suggestion of an insult. Hildy hoped that might change when they got to California. Ruby had a clue that California could be the place to find her father, but he may not have even known he had a daughter.

Grandma immediately put her arm around Ruby and welcomed her as if she were one of her own granddaughters.

Granddad playfully pulled on Hildy's long brown braids. She was the only one of the five girls who looked like her late mother. All the other girls, and even baby Joey, had light blond hair that almost looked white.

Granddad gently tugged at the white string Hildy had tied at the end of the braids. "Hildy, you got the prettiest hair."

Hildy gave her grandfather a quick hug, and they walked toward the house together in the dusk. The others followed, explaining about the car trouble and the need to get to California.

Inside the farmhouse, the coal oil lamps had already been

lit. They all stood around in the big kitchen and talked.

"If we don't get there in time," Elizabeth said with the serious wisdom of her years, "Dad's mean ol' boss will fire him. Then we won't have a job or the house Mr. Gridley promised we could live in."

Granddad held his right hand behind his ear and cocked his head. "Eh? What's that you said? Wait'll I get my hearing trumpet."

Hildy watched the white-haired man hurry through the big kitchen into the parlor. Even though she hadn't been in there since Christmas three years before, she remembered exactly what the parlor and the rest of the house looked like.

A big potbellied stove stood in one corner. Hildy and her sisters had warmed their pillows there at night; then they had followed their mother down the cold hallway as she led the way with a coal oil lamp that made scary black shadows.

Inside the bedroom with its ten-foot ceiling, the double bed, its brass headboard glistening, stood well off the floor. A feather mattress lay on top of cotton ticking filled with straw. Whenever they came to visit, all five sisters slept head to toe under home-made quilts and comforters in that one double bed. In winter a hot flatiron, warmed on the kitchen range and wrapped in a towel, kept the bed warm.

Hildy's memories were interrupted by a clank of metal as Grandma Corrigan raised the stove lid with a wire-handled device and slid a few pieces of oak wood into the box. Hildy marveled that the leaping flames never seemed to burn the stout woman's wrinkled hands.

Grandma pointed to the galvanized bucket sitting on the side table. "Everybody take a glass of milk," she said. "I just pulled it up from the well, so it's nice and cold. I'll bake some biscuits and warm up the beans while y'all tell me what's been going on."

Joe Corrigan sighed. "The rest of you can talk, but I've got to borrow a lantern and see what I can do about fixing that car."

As Hildy's father went out the kitchen door, Granddad returned with his hearing trumpet. It was a long, curved metal tube with a flared end. Placing the smaller end against his right ear, he tipped the other end toward the family. "Now," he said in a loud voice, "somebody tell me what brings y'all out here unexpected-like."

By the time the family sat down in the straight-back hickory kitchen chairs to eat, Hildy and her family had explained everything.

Granddad laid his hearing trumpet on the table and smiled at Hildy. There had always been a special feeling between the two. "So you're gonna find a 'forever home,' are you?"

Hildy nodded firmly, helping herself to a biscuit. "We sure are."

Granddad smiled. "A house with enough land to grow a garden and maybe have some chickens or rabbits? And you'll never have to move again, eh?"

Bashful five-year-old Sarah had been silent until now, but after swallowing a gulp of milk, she spoke up. "An' a pet!" she cried in a ringing voice. "A kitty or puppy or something."

Grandma peered into the oven at a second pan of biscuits. "But if you don't get there in seven days, Joe's boss will give his job to someone else, right? And you'll not be able to stay in the house that goes with the job?"

Molly fed the baby a spoonful of homemade applesauce. "Joe says we mustn't blame Mr. Gridley. Times are hard on people like him, same's us. Having all that land makes him rich, but also strict."

Elizabeth shook her head, her light blond hair flying. "He's mean. I heard Dad talking about him when you and he didn't know I was listening. And Daddy says his son Don is even meaner."

"Elizabeth, mind your words!" her stepmother spoke sharply.

"Well, it's true," Elizabeth said, digging at her food with a fork.

"Enough!" Molly snapped. "Let's look on the bright side of things."

Ruby spoke up quickly. "I'm gonna find my pa," she told

them with pride. "I done got a pi'ture of him—leastwise, I think it's him." Producing a sepia-tone snapshot, she handed it across the table to Hildy's grandfather. "Ain't he a mighty handsome lookin' man?" she said loud enough so he could hear.

Granddad Corrigan put on his silver-rimmed round bifocal glasses and peered thoughtfully at the photo. "That he is, Ruby." He raised his pale blue eyes and looked tenderly at the girl. "I hope you find him. Hildy told me about your family while she was visiting here a few Christmases back."

Ruby whirled to face Hildy, her eyes snapping. "What've ye been a-tellin' 'bout me?" she demanded.

Hildy had learned to speak softly to calm her sensitive cousin. "Nothing for you to get upset about, Ruby," she assured her.

Grandma turned from the stove, small beads of perspiration showing on her upper lip. "That's the truth, Ruby. Hildy loves you and would never do anything to hurt you. You must know that."

There was a moment's silence; then Ruby nodded and glanced at Hildy. "Reckon I do," she admitted in a small voice.

After dinner Hildy drew water from the cistern near the back porch and filled a graniteware pan. She set it on the stone that served as a step down from the screen door, and her sisters sat on the top step and washed their feet.

As Hildy stood in the soft, warm June night, dreamily listening to the whippoorwills call, she could smell the pleasant aroma of the nearby smokehouse, where her grandparents cured hog meat. Then her eyes lifted to the harness shed, and she could see her father's shadow bent over the Essex, working by lantern light.

Just then Ruby came out onto the porch, interrupting Hildy's thoughts. "Ye reckon he's gonna be able to fix it so's we kin git to Californy in time?"

"I'm praying so," Hildy replied.

"Prayin's a good idea," Grandma said behind them, just inside the screen door. "Now, Molly says all of you except Hildy and Ruby should be in bed."

The four younger girls, groaning in protest, finished drying their feet and walked slowly into the kitchen. Through the screen, Hildy saw her stepmother light a second coal oil lamp and start toward the bedrooms.

Ruby picked up the graniteware pan and threw the dirty water in a wide circular pattern across the dusty backyard. "It's twenty-five hunnert miles to Californy, yore paw says. I never was much good at fig'ers, but I done worked it out. That's more'n three hunnert miles a day. I mean, if'n we'uns air gonna make it on time."

"We'll make it," Hildy stated grimly. She poured some more water from the cistern bucket into the pan. "Now wash your feet so I can do mine. We're going to need a good night's sleep so we can start bright and early tomorrow."

A few minutes later, feet freshly washed, the two girls sat with Hildy's grandparents and Molly in the parlor. Grandma Corrigan's fingers moved quickly, mending her husband's gray work socks.

Hildy stared at the wall telephone. People who had a telephone in their home had to be fairly well-to-do even before the Depression started five years before. Now, like most people, her grandparents were just getting by.

Granddad leaned toward Hildy and adjusted his hearing trumpet so the flared end reached toward her. "You got any boyfriends yet?" he asked with a teasing smile.

Ruby grinned and bent toward the trumpet. "Ask her 'bout Spud."

Hildy swatted playfully at her cousin.

Granddad chuckled. "Spud? Is he a potato?"

"Aw, Granddad," Hildy protested, fidgeting in her chair. "That's not his real name. And he's not my boyfriend. He's just a boy we met."

Ruby nudged her cousin. "Show 'em the dictionary Spud gave ye."

Embarrassed, Hildy slouched down in her chair. "Let's talk about something else or I'm going to bed."

Grandma repositioned the darning egg in the sock she was

mending. "Now you two leave Hildy be," she scolded.

Ruby wouldn't quit. "Hildy's learnin' new words outta that dictionary ev'ry day, and she says she's gonna git real edjacated."

"Educated, huh?" Grandma said, lifting her gentle hazel eyes to her oldest granddaughter. "Then what d'you want to be when you grow up, Hildy?"

The girl shrugged. "I don't know for sure. A teacher, maybe."

Granddad clapped his hands. "You'd be a good one, too." He nodded vigorously.

Grandma continued moving her needle surely, automatically across the darning egg. "The important thing is to find out what the Lord wants you to do. Then, when things go bad, remember that the Bible says to trust in the Lord, and don't try to understand everything yourself. That's what makes Edgar and me get by even though these hard times keep hangin' on so long."

Hildy nodded, remembering how she had quit trusting God when her mother died. Only recently had Hildy recommitted herself to a life of faith. She felt sure that her family's future was in California. And she was trusting God to work things out.

Granddad had set his hearing trumpet on the floor beside him, but he seemed to understand his wife's words. "There comes a time when some things can't be explained. But we must never lose hope or faith. It's how people look at life that makes a difference."

His wife nodded. "Losing faith is what defeats people. Always remember that, girls. What you believe is as important as what you do. That's what you'll find for yourself when you look for this 'forever home' you want."

Hildy started to reply, but just then her father came through the door. One look at his discouraged face told her the bad news.

"The car's totally useless," he announced. "There's no way we can get to California now."

CHAPTER
TWO
—
BUGGY RIDE TO HOPE

O h, Daddy, don't say that!" Hildy exclaimed.
Her father was tired and in no mood to be patient. "It's no use, I tell you!" he snapped. Then he stalked out of the house and into the night.

Molly handed the sleeping baby to Hildy and followed her husband outside. A hushed discussion followed among the older girls and their grandparents. Hildy was too heartsick to say much.

Finally her grandmother said, "Hildy, since Joey's asleep, I'll put him down for the night while you two run to the outhouse and then go to your room and get some rest. Things will look better in the morning."

Granddad nodded. "Remember what we told you." He tugged gently at Hildy's long braids.

Taking the lantern, the girls made their way past the cistern, the well, and the smokehouse to the little house out in back. When they returned, they brushed the dust from their bare feet, blew out the lantern, and followed Grandma Corrigan. She carried a coal oil lamp high, leading the way down the long hallway.

Scary black shadows leaped away from the light as though they were trying to hide. When Hildy was little she had been afraid of those shadows. Now they seemed afraid of her, much like the way she was now feeling about her family's future.

In the high-ceilinged bedroom, the old woman kissed Hildy on the cheek, patted Ruby on the shoulder and left the light for them to undress by. Hildy sat before the walnut dresser and automatically loosened her braids, aching inside with disappointment.

Ruby stepped out of her plain cotton dress and stood in her underclothes made from flour sacks. The back still had the faint wording, *Best in the west*. Ruby reached carefully under the high bed with her bare foot and shoved the white porcelain chamber pot out of the way. Then she gave a little jump to land sitting upon the high bed.

"We cain't give up, Hildy. We jist cain't. I gotta find my pa— I mean, if'n it's really him."

"We'll get to California somehow," Hildy said with the stubbornness that was both her weakness and her strength. She started brushing out her hair, which cascaded down her back. "Soon's I finish this, let's pray about it."

"I still ain't much on prayin'," Ruby protested. "Ye know that."

"Then I'll do it for both of us."

Hildy gave her hair another quick stroke, then blew out the lamp and knelt by the bed. "Lord," she began, her words sounding soft and warm in the darkness, "I believe our home is in California. I'm going to trust you to help us get there. Now please help my daddy."

After ending her simple, direct prayer, Hildy stood up and slid under the sheet beside her cousin. It was nice to have only two in a bed. Often, all six girls shared a bed. Elizabeth regularly slept beside Hildy and Ruby with their feet toward Martha and Sarah. The trouble with that arrangement was that Martha, a restless sleeper, often scratched Hildy with her long toenails. Iola, the smallest, usually slept at the foot of the bed. But here

Hildy's grandparents had another bedroom where the four other sisters were already asleep.

Hildy stared, unseeing, at the high ceiling and settled into the soft mattress made of goose feathers plucked from the farm's own geese. If the girls' bodies hadn't held the mattress down, it would have rolled inward, almost covering them.

"You asleep?" Hildy whispered after a while.

"No." Ruby's voice sounded as sad as Hildy felt.

"We've got to talk Daddy into not giving up."

"We done tried that. Ye heerd him. He says the Essex's wuthless and cain't be traded in. 'Sides, he's only got fifty dollars cash fer buyin' another car."

Hildy rolled over to face her cousin, though she couldn't see her in the darkness. The straw ticking between the mattress and the bed's slat board frames sounded louder than Hildy remembered. "California . . ." she murmured dreamily. "I hear it's really special there. I'm sure we'll find a place to live forever when we get there."

"Ye said *when*, not *if'n* we git thar."

"We'll get there. You'll see. Remember what Granddad said about trust?"

The girls fell silent and finally slept.

By midmorning the next day, Hildy's determined attitude had persuaded her father to try again.

"Okay, okay!" he said reluctantly, looking around at all his family. "I agree. We've already got a place to stay and a job in California if we can get there in time. Here, we've got nothing. But to get there, we've got to have another car."

He turned to his father. "Papa, since the Essex won't run, would you let me borrow the horse and buggy? I'll ride into town and see if I can buy a used car for fifty dollars."

Granddad understood and nodded for him to go ahead.

Hildy jumped up and down. "Thanks, Daddy!" she exclaimed. "May I go with you?"

"And me?" Ruby cried.

"Me! Me!" the other sisters echoed.

Joe Corrigan's eyes were still bloodshot from lack of sleep. Hildy suspected that even after nearly a week of day-and-night driving from California to Illinois, he still hadn't slept much the night before.

He scratched his head. "There's only room for one in the buggy besides me. Hildy, because you're the oldest, you'd better come along. If I buy a car, you'll have to drive the mare back here."

A chorus of disappointment rose from the others, but Hildy wasn't surprised at her favored position. Her father often took her with him.

Sometimes Hildy wished she were more of a tomboy like Ruby because then she might have been a substitute for the older son her father didn't have. But now as they headed for town, she set her mind to make sure they returned with a vehicle that would make the trip in the time remaining.

Hildy enjoyed riding behind ol' Dixie again. The bay mare was probably fifteen years old now and gentle enough that her father allowed Hildy to take the reins. She didn't need the buggy whip, but she lifted it from its socket and swung it absently in the air. There was a good smell about a horse, Hildy thought. As the animal plodded toward town, the narrow iron rim on the red-spoked buggy crunched on the rocky road.

"Daddy?" Hildy replaced the whip in its socket and dropped the reins across the front of the buggy.

"Huh?"

"Promise me something?"

"What?"

"You won't lose your temper."

He reached over and playfully fingered the end of her long brown braid. "Hildy, you know I'm an easygoing guy. Why would you ask me a thing like that?"

"Because you've got a lot of problems right now, and sometimes you get mad real easy."

He looked into her eyes and smiled. "I won't lose my temper."

Hildy sighed and leaned over to give him a quick kiss. "Thanks."

Joe Corrigan kept his word for three frustrating hours as he approached car dealers who didn't have anything affordable.

At the last place, when her father couldn't make a deal, he stomped off, shouting angrily at the salesman. "You bunch of horse thieves!" he yelled. "Kick a man when he's down."

Hildy placed her foot on the buggy step and reached up to pull herself into the seat. Her insides twisted tightly, and her stomach hurt. She turned imploring blue eyes on her father. "Daddy, you promised."

"Crooks," her father muttered as he untied the horse from the hitching rail that stood at the curb between two automobiles. "Try to sell me those rolling junk piles for top dollar. Well, I'm an ol' horse trader from a-way back, and they can't cheat me!"

He pulled himself into the buggy so fast that the vehicle tipped sharply toward him. Grabbing the reins, he clucked to the mare. "Back up, Dixie. Let's go home."

Hildy turned anguished eyes toward the June sky. The sun slid behind a cloud, casting a deeper gloom over the girl. A storm seemed to be gathering. Her heart did flip-flops as she remembered the recent storm when lightning had struck the horse on which she was riding. Hildy hadn't felt a thing, but she realized how close she had come to dying.

The mare finished backing up and turned her head in response to the reins. Her iron-shod hooves made sharp sounds on the paved street as Hildy's father slapped the lines across her rump. Dixie increased her pace to a fast walk, moving through the town's mixture of horses, wagons, cars, and trucks.

Hildy's eyes filled with unwanted tears. She blinked them back, fighting doubt. *God let me down once when Mom died. Is He going to disappoint me again?*

Her father's angry voice interrupted her thoughts. "It's probably just as well," he said bitterly. "Ol' man Gridley's about the o'neriest boss I ever had. Well, I guess his son's worse than he is."

Hildy thought she had tried everything she knew to encourage her father, but nothing worked. Then she thought of something else. "Daddy, what about Ruby's father?"

"What about him?"

"She told you about finding a last-known address in California. Remember?"

"I remember. Place called Grizzly Gulch."

"You been there?"

"No, but I know where it is. It's one of those ghost towns from the Gold Rush of 1849. Not much there anymore."

"Is it far from Lone River?"

"Maybe an hour's ride up into the Mother Lode foothills."

"Ruby's determined to go to California and find her father, whether we go on or not."

"Crazy girl."

Hildy watched the mare turn onto the dirt road that ran through the residential district on the edge of town. "She was counting on going with us."

"Well, I'm sorry for her, but without a car, we're not going. And neither is she."

"I think she'll go on, no matter what you or I say."

"She should go back to the Ozarks where she belongs."

"She doesn't belong there any more than I do."

"It doesn't matter where we are, Hildy. One place's as good as another if I've got a job."

"You've got a job in California," Hildy reminded him mildly.

Her father's temper flashed. "Yes, but we don't have a car or a way to get there!" he shouted. "Now, forget about California." He reached for the buggy whip and gave the mare a sharp flip.

Startled, Dixie turned her head and looked at him.

Hildy's eyes widened. *I'll bet no whip has touched that horse in years*, she thought.

Still, Dixie broke into a trot down the house-lined street.

Hildy swallowed her disappointment and stared gloomily through the line of maple trees that shaded the front lawns.

Sunlight reflected off the purple-colored glass pieces that people used to decorate the front porch posts of their stucco homes.

It's no use, her mind told her. But her spirit urged, *Don't give up*.

The mare moved over slightly to pass a long gray touring car parked at the curb in front of an expensive two-story frame house. Hildy unconsciously read a sign in the car's back window: For Sale by Owner.

Suddenly she sat upright and stared at the sign. "Daddy, look!" She pointed.

"Too expensive."

"Couldn't we at least stop and ask the price? Look. There's somebody putting the hood down. Probably the owner. Please?"

"Oh, all right." Joe Corrigan pulled on the reins. "Whoa, Dixie. Whoa, now."

As the horse slowed, blowing noisily through her nostrils and tossing her head, Hildy studied the car. The buggy stopped beside the car, and the man at the engine turned and nodded with a smile.

"Afternoon," said the slender man with a pencil-thin moustache. He wore a silk shirt, felt snap-brim hat, and three-piece navy blue suit. Everything about him suggested that he was a well-to-do business or professional man.

"Howdy," Joe Corrigan replied with a somber nod.

Hildy forced a big smile. "Hello," she greeted. "Nice-looking car."

Her father shot a warning glance, and Hildy remembered too late what her father had said about trading for horses or cars: "Never say anything nice; just find the faults. That's the only way to make a person come down on his price."

Hildy's father still sat in the buggy, reins lightly held in his strong hands. "Start 'er up," he said to the man.

"Motor's already running, Mister."

A surprised look came into Joe Corrigan's eyes, but he quickly masked it. Slowly, he got down from the buggy, and Hildy followed.

Hildy's father studied the car thoughtfully. "How much?" he asked.

"She's worth four hundred dollars, but I'll take two."

"Two hun—?" Joe Corrigan's face showed anger; then he threw back his head and laughed. "For that? Mister, that's a 1926 Lexington Minuteman Six, and they don't make them anymore!"

"A '27 Lexington Minuteman Six," the owner corrected, flushing slightly at the laughter. "Best car I ever owned."

"I don't want to buy your car troubles."

"There's not a thing wrong with this car," the man replied defensively. "Why, not six months ago I sent it back to the factory for a complete overhaul and had it repainted with enamel. But I don't need it anymore. That's the only reason I'm parting with it."

"Probably a gas hog," Hildy's father muttered.

The man seemed not to hear. He pointed, speaking rapidly. "Two mufflers—one for every three cylinders—so it runs quiet. And it's a Phaeton, so you can fold the top down and ride in the sunshine if you want. Lots of room inside for your daughter here and more if there's more to your family."

He raised a highly polished leather shoe and rested it on the running board. "Look at these running boards," he said proudly. "Nearly two feet wide with folding gates. You can carry as much on the running boards as inside. Say, why don't you just slide under the wheel and see how it feels?"

Hildy held her breath while her father considered the offer.

Slowly he shook his head. "Not worth your asking price, Mister. Sorry." He turned back to the buggy.

Hildy's hopes sagged. She almost groaned.

"Wait!" the owner cried. "It's got two spare tires and a compressor to pump them up if you have a flat."

Joe Corrigan hesitated, his foot on the buggy's step.

Hildy whispered behind him, "You've got nothing to lose. Make him an offer."

"Okay," he whispered back. "I'll make one try."

Hildy turned away and lifted her eyes to the sky. The sun was shining, but the clouds were still rolling in. "Please," she whispered. "Please, Lord!"

Her father raised his voice. "I got fifty dollars cash to my name. Take it or leave it."

Hildy anxiously watched the other man's face. He half closed his eyes, then shrugged. "I'm cheating myself, but I don't need the car. Give me the money," he said.

Hildy didn't mean to shout, but a glad cry burst out. "Yipppee! We're going to California!"

Then she remembered there were only six days left to cover twenty-five hundred miles.

Chapter Three

ON THE ROAD AGAIN

Hildy felt proud that her father let her drive the horse and buggy home alone while he followed in the glistening Lexington Minuteman. In her excitement she wanted to touch the mare lightly with the whip to urge her into a faster gait. But Hildy contented herself with slapping the lines vigorously on the bay's flanks and calling out encouragement.

"Giddyap there, Dixie! Faster! Faster! The quicker we get back to Granddad's, the sooner we can pack the new car and be on our way to California!"

The horse turned and seemed to give her a reproving look.

Hildy felt a little guilty. "Oh, all right," she muttered. "I know you're old and going as fast as you can. Now turn around and keep your eyes on the road so you don't stumble and fall."

It was ten miles from town to Granddad Corrigan's farm. Hildy remembered the winter three years before when it had taken four hours to make this same trip. They were riding in the spring wagon and the dirt road was mostly mud mixed with snow. This buggy was faster than the wagon, but it was still a fairly long ride, and Hildy sang to herself to pass the time.

The mare didn't really need Hildy's guidance on the reins. Dixie knew the way home, and she took it with right good will. When the buggy's iron-rimmed wheels crunched on the dry ruts as they turned into the farm, four eager tow-headed sisters rushed to meet Hildy.

"Are we going?" Elizabeth shouted.

"Who's in the car?" Martha asked.

Sarah demanded, "Where's Daddy?"

"How come you're driving the horsie?" little Iola inquired. "I don't get to drive the horsie."

Hildy pulled back on the reins. "Whoa, Dixie," she called softly. As the mare stopped, blowing noisily through her nostrils, Hildy grinned down at her sisters. "Yes, we're going! That's Daddy following in his new car!"

"Whoopee!" Elizabeth cried, turning back toward the farmhouse. "Molly, we're going! We're going!"

The three younger sisters joyfully dashed after her, screaming, "Granddad! Grandma! We're going!"

Ruby ran out on the back porch, letting the screen door bang loudly. She carried the baby, Joey, who was crying in fright at the unexpected commotion and sudden movements. "Hildy, ye tellin' the truth?" Ruby cried.

"It's true. Look, isn't Daddy's new car a beauty?"

After everyone from grandparents to the baby inspected and admired the car, they began packing everything they wouldn't need that night into the Lexington.

Then, in order to get some spending money for the long journey ahead, Joe Corrigan pulled his old car back into town and sold it for parts.

In the evening, the younger children were fed early and sent to bed. Then Hildy and Ruby sat in the parlor and talked softly while the adults chattered away in the kitchen.

"Six full days to git thar," Ruby said thoughtfully.

"Got to be there by Saturday morning," Hildy agreed, "but we can make it."

"Less'n we have car trouble or somethin'."

Hildy turned quickly. "Don't talk like that," she said sharply. "We're going to make it!"

"Well, we done lost a full day a'ready," Ruby muttered, "but I want to git to Californy more'n anybody. Nobody knows what it's like, not knowin' if'n ye got a pa or not."

Hildy reached out and lightly touched her cousin's arm. "We'll get there, and I really do hope you find him." Hildy's eyes surveyed the room and she changed the subject. "This might be the last time I ever see this place," she said softly.

Hildy tried to etch on her memory how everything looked: the telephone on the wall with its crank and bells and protruding mouthpiece, the large dining room table with its needle-pointed chair cushions, the door leading upstairs, the potbellied stove on the opposite side of the room, where her sisters often sprawled on a rug.

Ruby followed her gaze. "This's a mighty purdy place, ain't it? Nicer'n anythin' we ever had in the Ozarks."

Hildy nodded. "When I was here three Christmases ago— when Daddy was in Texas looking for work—Mom was still alive. And she and Grandma put up red and green Christmas bells right there." She pointed to the ceiling in the center of the room. "We didn't have any tree, just those bells. They were made out of paper and folded up flat after Christmas. I got a handkerchief that year. One plain white handkerchief."

Such a stark Christmas didn't seem strange to Ruby. She shrugged but didn't answer.

Hildy continued. "The little kids got some broken toys and dolls Grandma had left over from when Daddy and his brothers and sisters were little. Then all of us kids shared some hard Christmas candy and got one orange apiece. Mom said we were lucky to have that because of the hard times."

"Christmas ain't never been much to me, nohow," Ruby finally said.

Hildy was still lost in thought, remembering. "Joey wasn't born, of course. Iola was a baby, so she couldn't remember. I'm not sure whether the other girls can or not. We were all together except Daddy. He couldn't get home." Hildy said brightly, "But that's all in the past. Soon we'll all be together in California— the whole family, forever. Maybe in a big house like this."

"Think ye kin remember this place?" Ruby asked.

"It's the only place I expect to remember."

"Wish I had me a place I'd want to remember."

Hildy gave her cousin a hug. "It'll be different if you find your father. Then you'll always be together—finally—and you can make some new memories."

Ruby did not answer. Both girls lapsed into silence that lasted until the adults blew out the kitchen lamp and came into the parlor.

Hildy's father picked up the remaining lamp. "Bedtime, girls," he said. "We'll roll out before dawn and be on our way by daybreak."

Hildy was so excited she didn't remember falling asleep, but she was awakened by the rooster's first crowing. Sitting up in bed, she shook Ruby. "It's time!" She slid off the high bed and onto the floor, grabbing her clothes and putting them on quickly.

Then she stopped suddenly, hearing Joey's cry. "Oh no! Something's wrong with the baby!"

Ruby jumped out of bed and dressed hurriedly. When they were dressed, both girls raced down the hallway, through the parlor, and into the kitchen. One glance at Molly holding the fretting baby was enough. The situation was serious.

Hildy's stepmother glanced up at the girls. "Joey may be coming down with chicken pox."

"Chicken pox?" Hildy exclaimed, coming near to touch the crying baby's forehead. "You sure?"

"No," Molly said, "but the rest of the kids just got over them a couple weeks ago, so it's possible."

Hildy turned anguished eyes on her father. "Does that mean we can't start today?"

He nodded gravely. "We can't begin such a long trip until we know for sure what Joey's got."

"But if it is chicken pox, he'll be sick for days!"

"That's right, Hildy. But there's nothing we can do but wait and see."

The morning dragged while everyone waited anxiously. No one called a doctor. That wasn't done except in real emergencies.

To keep her mind off their delay, Hildy volunteered to help her grandmother feed the reddish-colored chickens and gray guinea hens that ran free in the yard. As she was scattering the grain, Hildy heard a church bell faintly in the distance, and a strange longing came over her.

Grandma Corrigan looked up. "That's to call people to Sunday school and church," she said. "It also rings when someone dies. One ring for each year of the person's life."

"How come we can hear it way out here, Grandma?"

"Wind's right, I guess. You still go to church, Hildy?"

Hildy watched the Rhode Island red rooster and his hens happily clucking and pecking at the grain in the dirt. "I stopped for a while after Mom died, but recently, I . . . well, I'm going back regularly when we get settled in California."

"I'm glad," her grandmother replied, emptying the pan of the last bits of grain. "There comes a time in everybody's life when they need Someone greater than they are to help them through."

The two started for the back porch before Hildy spoke again. "How come Daddy doesn't go to church? When Mom was alive, she kept asking him to go with her . . . us . . . but he wouldn't."

"I don't rightly know, Hildy. He went when he was little. Went to Christian Endeavor, too, when he was growing up, but something happened after he came home from the war. I don't know what, really. I keep praying. Someday, he'll come back, I'm sure."

For the first time, Hildy realized that her grandmother carried a heavy load of concern about her son, and Hildy couldn't help but feel sad.

At last the long day ended. And that night Hildy fretted as she sat on the back stoop and washed her feet. "Sure hope Joey's okay in the morning," she told Ruby.

"Me, too." Ruby absently snatched at a firefly as it floated silently by. "Otherwise, I'm a-goin' by myself. Got to find my pa."

"Joey didn't get any worse today, so I'm going to pray he'll be okay to travel tomorrow."

The next morning, Hildy awakened at the rooster's crowing and sat up, listening. Joey wasn't crying. Hildy jumped out of bed and ran on silent bare feet to the kitchen where Molly was already feeding the baby.

Molly smiled tiredly. "Whatever Joey had is gone. Your father says we're starting for California today."

A lot of rushing around followed, and in no time at all, the last items, including the lunch Grandma had made for them, were packed into the car or onto the wide running boards. Then the hurried goodbyes began.

"Goodbye, Grandma," Hildy said, kissing her grandmother's cheek. "I love you."

"Remember what I told you about trusting," Grandma told her.

Hildy nodded and turned to Granddad. "'Bye," she whispered. "I'll write when we get settled."

He playfully tugged on her long brown braids. "God bless you," he said softly. Then reaching into his deep pocket, he took out a small well-worn Bible and pressed it into her hands. "Here," he said. "Your grandma and I want you to have this. It belonged to my father, so it's special." He winked.

Hildy swallowed hard, finally managing a soft *thank you* before crawling into the backseat with Ruby, Elizabeth, Martha, Sarah and Iola.

"Goodbye, goodbye!" everyone called as the Lexington Minuteman pulled away from the Corrigan farm, heading west.

It was barely sunup when Joe Corrigan turned in the front seat where Molly sat beside him holding the sleeping baby. "Well," he said, "we're almost broke, and we're twenty-five hundred miles from California with five days to get there. We can make it by driving day and night, the kids sleeping in the car."

Hildy didn't say anything, but she wondered if her father was rested enough to drive so hard for so long. *He certainly hasn't had much sleep with the sick baby crying.*

As they crossed into Missouri on the Lincoln Highway, Hildy's father turned to his wife and smiled. "This car's running like a railroader's watch," he said. "I hope it keeps up. We didn't have time to road test it."

Ruby leaned forward against the backseat. "How're we gonna git to Californy, Uncle Joe?"

"The Lincoln Highway runs straight across the country, so we'll just stay on it most of the way," he explained. "Through Missouri, Kansas, Nebraska, Wyoming, Colorado, Utah, Nevada, then California."

Little Iola leaned forward, her blue eyes large as silver dollars. "Is that far?" she asked.

Her father laughed. "It's far enough. But if we have any trouble on the road, we'll just stop and work until we get money to go on. If we don't earn enough, guess we can go back to Texas instead of on to California. I always liked Texas."

Hildy's heart jumped. "Oh, Daddy, we can't do that!"

"Might have to, sweetheart."

"I remember picking cotton down there in the panhandle. I don't ever want to do that again."

"Then let's hope this Lexington doesn't give us any trouble and we get to California by Friday morning." Her father sounded more positive than before.

The big car continued steadily westward, hour after hour. At noon, the family picnicked by the roadside, then drove on, chasing the sun all afternoon.

Hildy studied the many nice houses they passed. *No,* she told herself, *none of those is what I want our "forever home" to look like.*

When darkness fell, the kids got cranky, squabbling over the crowded conditions and lack of rest stops. But the touring car continued on and on, westward. Eventually, all except Hildy fell into a tired sleep.

Suddenly, Hildy felt the car swerve. She glanced up in alarm. Her father whipped the steering wheel, swinging the Lexington back onto the road.

Molly put her arm on her husband's shoulder. "What happened, Joe?"

"Guess I must've dozed off."

"Joe," Molly whispered urgently, "you can't drive safely day and night with all your family in the car. I wish I knew how to drive. We're going to have to stop at a tourist cabin so you can get some rest."

"I can't do that, Molly. You know old man Gridley won't hold my job if I'm not there by Friday."

Hildy leaned forward. "That's better than having a wreck, Daddy."

As her father nodded, Hildy sank back into the seat. *I just hope we still get there on time!*

CHAPTER
FOUR

CAR TROUBLE

The next day turned into a tiring twelve-hour drive for a crowded carload of cranky kids. Since Molly didn't drive, her husband stayed at the wheel from shortly after daybreak until well after dark.

Hildy and Ruby bore up well because every mile took them closer to California and the realization of their dreams. But when the other girls and Joey weren't sleeping, they cried, quarreled, and fussed endlessly in spite of Hildy's efforts to entertain them with games, stories, and songs.

The four younger sisters kept asking, "Are we there yet?" and Ruby muttered, "Ain't they no way a body kin make them young'uns hesh up 'til we git thar?"

Hildy tried unsuccessfully. Thinking Elizabeth and Martha were old enough to understand, she repeatedly explained to them how long the trip would take. "Daddy's original plan was to drive the twenty-five hundred miles in seven days," she said. "That meant he had to average about three hundred sixty miles a day. Then we lost two days because of the car trouble and Joey getting sick."

Her sisters frowned in confusion and Hildy took a deep breath. "So that means Daddy had to increase his daily mileage to five hundred each day," she continued. "He says the best average speed he can make is only forty-five miles an hour on these dusty, rutted roads. And we're still a few days away from California."

Elizabeth and Martha only shook their heads and shrugged.

As the darkness settled, Joe Corrigan wearily stopped at a dollar-a-night tourist cabin, which was one big room with a kitchen. Hildy helped her stepmother prepare a quick meal on the wood-burning stove, but the exhausted children ate little before heading for bed.

Molly stopped them. "Wait'll I check for bedbugs," she said.

Hildy was glad the inspection showed none of the wingless, flat bloodsuckers so common in many houses and bedding. Her little sisters didn't care. They fell into bed and instantly went to sleep.

Early the next morning, when the family rolled out of bed, the younger children remained tired and cross. Breakfast was made quickly and eaten even faster. Then they all reloaded the car and took their places in the automobile.

Joe Corrigan slid under the steering wheel and hit the starter.

Nothing happened.

Hildy's heart skipped a beat. "What's the matter?" she asked.

"Not sure," her father answered. "Seems like a short or something." He pressed on the foot starter again. This time the motor leaped to life.

"Whew!" Hildy said with a sigh. She leaned back in the rear seat as her father steered the touring sedan out onto the street.

Stopping at a service station, he turned off the motor to gas up. Hildy noticed the price: twenty cents a gallon. After filling the gas tank and the canvas water bags on the front bumper, Joe Corrigan slipped back into the driver's seat.

Again, the car wouldn't start.

Hildy sensed a problem building, but before she could say

anything, the motor caught and held. In moments, they were rolling west again.

But Hildy couldn't relax.

Neither could Ruby. "Reckon it'll come a time when we stop and the engine won't start up no more?"

"It'll be all right," Hildy said with a conviction she didn't feel.

The day dragged on without the starter acting up again, so Hildy began to feel better. She played games with her sisters, like contests to see who could be the first to spot a license plate for a state other than the one through which they were passing.

For a while, with their father's help, they tried identifying cars. But some, like Ford, Chevrolet, Oldsmobile, and Dodge were easier than others like Whippets, Overlands, Stars, Moons, Graham-Paiges, Hudsons, and La Salles.

When Hildy's little sisters tired of that game, Hildy switched to "Who am I thinking of?" She wanted to use presidents and other famous people, but her sisters didn't know enough of those. So each child gave clues that helped identify one of their friends or relatives.

When Molly needed a rest from holding the baby in her lap, she passed him back to Hildy. Hildy enjoyed playing with her little brother, but he was so active and the car was so cramped that Hildy often handed Joey on to Ruby for a while.

Sometimes the younger sisters napped, leaning awkwardly against each other in the backseat. While they slept, Hildy produced the small pocket dictionary her friend Spud had given her. Hildy and Ruby had met the fourteen-year-old boy while they were traveling from Arkansas to Oklahoma. Ruby and Spud hadn't gotten along at all, but Hildy rather liked the knickers-clad Irish-American who loved big words.

Ruby noticed the dictionary and leaned over toward Hildy. "Ye reckon y'all ever see Spud agin?" she asked quietly.

Hildy finished sounding out a new word and shrugged. "Maybe."

"Are ye a-learnin' them new words ever' day so's ye kin

impress him if'n ye see him agin?"

"I'm learning these words for myself, Ruby."

Her cousin grinned and lightly punched Hildy's ribs. "Shore, ye air."

The weary travelers continued westward, spending the third night at a run-down tourist cabin with a kerosene kitchen stove instead of a wood-burning one. Molly had a busy time fighting bedbugs before she felt it was safe for the children to sleep.

That night Hildy announced, "We're right on schedule. We can still make it by Saturday if we don't have any more car trouble. Then Mr. Gridley can't fire Daddy."

Sometimes, when they were driving and the other kids were asleep in a tangled mass of arms and legs beside her, Hildy gazed down at the bumpy, unpaved road and repeated the same silent prayer. "Please, Lord, please!"

Sometimes she rocked back and forth, silently chanting to herself on each forward swing of her body. "Go. Go. Go, Lexington Minuteman car, Go!"

In the morning the big touring car started without any trouble, and the family continued to roll steadily west, following the Lincoln Highway. As they passed through each state, Hildy marked them off on the map in the back of Spud's dictionary. Soon they left the plains and climbed into the Rocky Mountains.

Hildy thoughtfully reviewed where they had been and where they yet had to go. "Illinois, Missouri, Kansas, up to Nebraska, and now Colorado. Then we'll go just inside Wyoming, across Utah, and Nevada into California. We'll make it by Saturday morning—I hope."

The Rockies' twisting, narrow mountain roads had no guard rails, and Hildy kept swallowing hard as she peered anxiously down the steep canyons.

Ruby stared out the window, her eyes growing wide. "If'n we roll down thar," she muttered, "we won't stop 'til we bump up agin' China!"

Hildy was too scared to appreciate her cousin's humor.

Her father glanced back at them. "Did you girls see that?" he asked in an amused tone.

"See what?" they asked together.

"Why, the last curve we went around was so sharp our head-lights almost bumped into our taillights," he teased.

"Oh, Daddy," Hildy protested. "That's not funny."

As he started around another sharp curve, he sounded his horn as the law required. "Well, maybe not, but I'd rather be laughing than scaring myself. Wouldn't you?"

Hildy agreed, but she breathed a silent prayer for safety as the car climbed higher into the Rockies.

With the many switchbacks and hairpin curves, the kids soon began to feel queasy. When the car came to a wide enough spot, Hildy's father pulled off the narrow road to let them get some fresh air. Although he didn't say anything about the apparent short in the starter, Hildy felt relieved that he left the motor running.

Another car facing east had already stopped at the same spot. A beat-up mattress hugged the roof of the Model T Ford. About a dozen kids and a woman sat inside the car while a skinny man in faded, tattered overalls and a gray hat checked the radiator under the raised hood.

Hildy's father walked toward the man. "Where you headed, Mister?" he called.

The stranger looked up. "Back to Texas," he replied with a drawl. "From Californy."

As Hildy opened the door and deeply breathed the cooler mountain air, she felt a little less sick. She drifted closer to hear the conversation, wondering why anyone would leave the promised land of California.

Her father wiped his brow with his shirt sleeve. "We're heading out there now. How come you didn't like California?"

"Mister, if'n I was you, I'd turn around raht now and head back to wherever y'all come from," the skinny man replied. "But to answer yore question: we all liked it, raht enough. They's just already too many of us floodin' into Californy to suit them as already lives there."

He slammed down the hood of his car and wiped his hands on his overalls. "Ye never heerd so many names called a body, like *Okie* and *Arky*. Didn't matter none that we was Texans. To them, we was all Okies or Arkies an' about as welcome as a mad dog at a Sunday school picnic."

Hildy frowned. "Those don't sound like such terrible names."

"Oh, it ain't the words so much as the hate that's in them. So they done run us off. See?"

The man pulled off his grimy gray hat and showed them a nasty welt on his head. "Got that from a pick handle," he said. "Since that was the third time somebody beat up on me fer tryin' to work, I took the hint. Goin' back where folks is friendly-like."

Hildy took a step toward him. "You're just saying that to scare us from going on," she challenged.

The skinny man turned sad brown eyes on her and shook his head. "Wisht I was, little girl, but I shore ain't. Like I said, if'n I was yore daddy, I'd turn my car around afore somebody busts his head and maybe hurts ye kids, too."

Hildy was relieved when her father called the kids back into the Lexington and again headed west.

After a few minutes of driving in silence, her father finally spoke. "I know some people who've lived in California a long time don't like all the thousands of people now pouring in looking for work," he said thoughtfully. "My boss, Mr. Gridley, is one of them. His son Don's another. Don hates everybody who wasn't born in Lone River as he was. But Mr. Gridley gave me a job, which I've still got."

Ruby nudged Hildy. "He has," she whispered, "if'n he kin git thar in time."

"We're doing fine," Hildy replied, annoyed. "The car's running perfectly."

"Then how come yore daddy didn't turn off the engine whilst he stopped back thar?"

Hildy leaned forward across the front seat. "Daddy, is the car going to start again if you turn the motor off?"

"I'm not taking any chances, sweetheart. When we get out of these mountains, I'll find a garage and see if that starter short can be fixed. We won't stop until then."

But as they started down out of the Wasatch Range of the Rockies toward Salt Lake City, Joe Corrigan tensed noticeably behind the wheel. "This car handles like it has a low tire," he announced with a sigh.

Hildy remained calm, knowing that the Lexington had two unused spares.

When her father found a place wide enough, he pulled off the mountain road to inspect the tires. After a few seconds he walked over to the passenger side and leaned in to talk to his wife. "Left rear tire's low, Molly. You'll have to get out so I can pump it up. The rest of you may's well get out and stretch your legs, too, but stay close."

Hildy was too anxious to reach California to care much about looking at the scenery with the rest of the kids and Molly. Barely noticing the dark green evergreens set against the pale blue mountain peaks surrounding them, Hildy turned her attention to her father as he removed the front seat.

"What're you doing?" she asked.

"Getting to the compressor, see?" He pointed. "I start it up, like this." A low hum sounded as the compressor motor started. "Then I use this short silver handle on the floorboard beside the hand brake and throw the compressor into gear. Now I take this long red rubber hose and pump up the low tire."

Hildy watched with fascination. Her limited experience with flat tires on cars had been with a Model T that had a hand pump to blow up the flat. The Lexington's red rubber hose reached all four tires.

When the low tire was pumped up, Joe Corrigan put the hose away and replaced the seat. "That'll hold us until we find a service station where I can have the tire fixed," he announced. "Everybody back in the car. Let's go."

As he continued driving through the Wasatch Range of the Rockies toward Salt Lake, he pulled into the first garage he saw.

Hildy noticed that there were tourist cabins behind. She and Ruby got out of the car and stood by Hildy's father as he talked to the mechanic about the tire and starter.

The mechanic wiped his hands on a red rag and squinted at the Lexington. "Tire's no problem, but the starter's another matter. They don't make this car anymore, so I don't have a part. Have to send back east for it."

Hildy's heart sank.

Her father sighed loudly. "How long'll that take?"

"Maybe a month."

"A month?" Hildy cried.

The man shrugged. "You and your family can stay in my cabins until the part comes."

Hildy groaned in dismay, and Ruby cried, "Now we ain't never gonna make it to Californy on time!"

CHAPTER
FIVE

A TRICK WITH A HOLE
IN IT

Hildy felt heartsick as she watched her father consider the mechanic's words.

"A month to get the part, you say, Mister?" he asked.

"About. Yep. But your family'll be comfortable over there in my modern tourist cabins. First class, but reasonable."

Joe Corrigan nodded. "I'll think on that a bit while you fix the tire and fill the gas tank."

As the mechanic walked away, Hildy thought she saw a look of triumph on his face. She turned to her father anxiously. "What'll we do now?"

Her father frowned as though deep in thought. He didn't answer her. Instead, he raised his voice and called to the mechanic. "You got a piece of copper wire about two feet long?"

"Sure. Right over there against the wall. Help yourself."

"How much?"

"Nothing."

"Much obliged," Mr. Corrigan replied.

Hildy and Ruby followed him while he picked up a piece of glistening copper wire, then headed back for the car. Hildy pulled on her father's shirt sleeve. "What're you going to do?" she asked.

Her father grinned and winked. "Watch and I'll show you a trick with a hole in it."

That was his favorite expression for something he didn't intend to tell. She watched as he raised the hood, reached down, and pulled the old wire away from the starter.

"Daddy!" she cried in dismay. "What've you done?"

"Know in a few minutes," he said, his voice muffled under the hood. "Why don't you girls go help Molly look after the kids?"

Hildy and Ruby obeyed.

Soon the mechanic finished patching the tire and rolled it back to Mr. Corrigan. "What d'ya say, Mister? Want to stay in my cabins while I order that part?"

"I'm obliged to you," Joe Corrigan replied. He lowered the hood and reached into his pocket. "How much for the tire and gas?"

Hildy kept an eye on her father as he paid the mechanic.

"All right, everybody," Joe Corrigan called, "get aboard."

"Joe," Molly protested, "it won't do any good."

His expression didn't change as he walked around to the driver's side. "Get in if you're going to California with me."

Puzzled, Hildy and the others hurried into the long touring car. Hildy leaned forward to watch as her father reached for a switch on the dashboard.

"What're you doing?" she asked, knowing that he hadn't touched the starter button.

He half turned and grinned at her. "Shhh! I'm opening the cutout."

"The what?" Hildy asked.

"There're dual mufflers on this Lexington," her dad explained, "and they usually make the motor almost totally silent. But there's also a switch you can turn to bypass the mufflers.

Then the sound can go directly from the engine out the tailpipe. You can hear it for miles."

Again her father winked at her, and Hildy's excitement began to rise. He pulled the cutout knob and then stretched his foot toward the starter.

Rmmmmm! The car roared to life.

The mechanic whirled around in surprise. "Mister, how on earth did you do that?"

Joe Corrigan smiled. "Trade secret. I'm a bit of a mechanic myself."

"Well, you're a mighty good one!" the man exclaimed, shaking his head in wonder.

The mechanic stood there, staring, as the Lexington thundered out onto the road again. Over the roar, Hildy's father explained what he had done. "This car's got two switches for lights—one for the headlights and another for the taillights. So I connected the starter to the taillights. They'll stay on all the time, day and night, but that won't matter. We'll never again have to worry about the car starting."

Ruby let out a whoop. "Then we're gonna make it on time?"

"It's looking good," Hildy's father said, beginning to whistle a little tune.

Hildy wanted to sing for joy. She led her sisters in a series of happy songs as they drove through Salt Lake City and across the desert. Suddenly, Hildy stopped mid-song and turned toward her father in alarm. "What's that?" she demanded, cocking her head to listen.

"That's what a car sounds like on a cement road," he explained with a laugh. "There're seventeen miles of concrete highway outside of Salt Lake City—the only such place in the whole country."

"It's wonderful!" Hildy exclaimed. "And the car doesn't bounce or anything."

"Enjoy it while you can," her father replied. "Soon's it runs out, we hit some of the worst stretches of roads in all the west."

He was right. The seventeen miles of paved highway soon ended, and the Lexington bounced around on washboard roads that threatened to shake the car apart.

In the desert they drove at night because it was too hot to drive during the day. What few cars there were also traveled at night, poking their way along the corduroy roads that made headlights dance crazily.

When Hildy noticed her father speeding up and slowing down, she asked what he was doing.

"Trying to find the best speed for these rough roads," he said. "And I think I've found it—forty-five miles an hour."

Other cars crept along at five to ten miles an hour. And in the bright light of the full moon, Hildy could see the surprised faces of the people in the other cars when the Lexington Minuteman passed them doing forty-five.

As the rest of the kids slept in the backseat, Hildy leaned forward to be nearer her father. "What makes the roads so rough?" she asked.

"Wind and weather cuts away the softest sand, I guess, so only the hardest part of the road remains," her father answered. "That makes ruts or gullies where the sand was blown away. It's like driving over your stepmother's washboard, only worse because the ridges are so much higher. Guess that's why they call them washboard roads."

Satisfied with that answer, Hildy leaned back in the seat for a while and watched their progress out the windshield.

There were no towns in the desert, so Joe Corrigan occasionally stopped to let the kids take a short stroll. He always walked ahead of them with a flashlight to check for rattlesnakes, especially deadly sidewinders.

"They're small but poisonous," he told them. "They bury themselves in the sand so only their eyes show. Almost impossible to see that way."

Hildy wasn't as afraid of snakes as she was of the coyotes. Their mournful yips and howls in the night made her hair stand on end.

When the family came to a small desert community, they found that gasoline cost eighty cents a gallon and drinking water cost ten cents a glass. Everything was more expensive because it had to be hauled in from distant points.

After stopping to get some sleep, they traveled through the city of Reno, then crossed the last of the desert. On Friday night, they left Nevada behind.

Then Hildy's father turned off the Lincoln Highway he had followed all the way from Illinois and took Highway 40 toward Lake Tahoe. Only California had numbered roads, and these were paved. Hildy was asleep when the car pulled into the agriculture inspection station at the California border.

"Everybody out," her father announced.

The little kids and Joey grumbled and fussed, cranky from being awakened, but Molly and the older girls tried to calm them.

Uniformed inspectors took every item out of the Lexington to check for possible bugs or pests hitchhiking into the state where agriculture was tremendously important.

As soon as the inspectors finished their work, Joe Corrigan reloaded the car with the girls' help. Then they all got back in, and the little ones grumpily went back to sleep.

Hildy, however, was now wide awake, much too excited to sleep. She leaned forward. "Daddy, the moon's not up yet, but that looks like mountains out there."

"They *are* mountains, honey. The Sierra Nevada Mountains of California. Make the Ozarks seem like foothills, don't they? We'll be in them for a couple of hours; after that we'll drop down into the valley near Sacramento."

"How far is that from Lone River?"

"We'll be there before morning. So don't you worry. I'll still have my job and the house the boss promised."

After they had gotten well into the mountains, Mr. Corrigan stopped beside a natural waterfall. It wasn't very high—maybe twenty feet or so—but there was a steady cascade of delicious, cold water. At nearly seven thousand feet elevation, this water had been snow a few days before, Hildy's father explained.

After the long desert crossing, they all enjoyed washing the grime from their faces and hands. The kids laughed and splashed each other.

Hildy cupped her hands and drank and drank from the cold, refreshing water. She drank so much that she felt her stomach wouldn't hold any more. "I think I'm going to burst," she announced, "but it's so good! I'll remember this the rest of my life."

"Me, too," Ruby said, drying her hands on her skirt. She peered through the night into the valley just as the moon began easing over the mountains they would soon be leaving behind. "Reckon I'll find my pa down there?"

Hildy nodded. "I hope so."

After a few minutes, everyone piled into the car again, the usual head count was taken, and the family headed down the Sierras into the valley below. The younger children and Ruby slept, but Hildy stared out into the night, thinking, *I wonder when we'll see our "forever home." Maybe soon?*

With the mighty Sierras behind them, the car passed through the state capital at Sacramento and headed for Stockton. Hildy was surprised to find paved roads all the way. Except for the seventeen miles outside of Salt Lake City, they had traveled only dirt and gravel roads. *California really is the Promised Land!* Hildy thought.

And she became certain of that when her father stopped for gas in Stockton. She wanted to cheer when she learned that there was a gas war there. Gasoline was just six cents a gallon.

With a full tank, the touring sedan swung south into the great San Joaquin Valley.

Her father glanced back at Hildy in the darkened car. "We're almost there, Hildy." He spoke softly, but excitement edged his voice.

The moon started to set in the west as the Lexington turned east and headed back toward the Sierras. Hildy's father slowed at the outskirts of Lone River, the last town in the valley. The Sierra foothills started just east of the city limits.

Spying a cluster of tourist cabins, Hildy's father stopped and found the owner. But the grumpy old man with a long gray beard insisted that they pay a whole dollar for the night even though it was nearly over. When Hildy's dad paid the fee from his nearly depleted funds, the owner gave him a key.

The exhausted family unloaded the car, and the older children helped steer the crying, complaining younger children into the cabin. Molly was too tired to check the beds. She let all the kids collapse wherever they wanted.

When they were all settled, Hildy's father told her that he was going to go on ahead to make sure he got his job. "I'll work all day and be back about sunset," he promised.

Hildy walked with him to the car. "We made it, huh, Daddy?"

"We made it." He took her braids by the ends and gently fingered them. "You try to sleep. Here. Take this money and buy groceries for breakfast and lunch. That's about all the money we've got left. Be careful."

"I will," she promised.

"Help Molly with the kids, won't you?"

"Sure." Hildy kissed her father on the cheek.

When the Lexington had vanished down the quiet streets lined with great sycamores and Dutch elm trees, Hildy said a silent prayer and returned to the cabin.

Leaving her clothes on, she climbed into bed with Ruby but couldn't sleep. As Hildy listened to her cousin's even breathing, she hoped Ruby could find her father. Most of all, Hildy hoped her own father's mean boss had held the job and the house for them. After a while, she finally dozed off into a restless sleep.

Suddenly she awakened with a start and sat up. The sun was seeping through the roll-up window shades on the east, so Hildy knew it was still morning. Everyone was asleep except Molly. Hildy rubbed her eyes, then saw Molly hurry to the door, holding the sleeping baby. As Molly crossed the cabin's bare wooden floor in her nightgown, Hildy noticed that her hair was still mussed from sleep.

That's when Hildy heard the knock at the door. Sliding out of bed, she ran on silent bare feet to stand beside her stepmother.

Molly opened the door carefully. "Joe! What happened?"

Joe Corrigan's face was ashen under his beard stubble. The

weariness in his eyes was emphasized by slumped shoulders and a sad expression. "Come out where we won't wake the others," he said.

As Hildy and Molly stepped outside, Hildy felt the cool morning breeze on her cheeks. Then a sudden deep chill swept over her entire body.

"He fired me." Joe Corrigan's voice was controlled but edged with anger.

"Oh, Daddy, no!"

"Gridley said I was supposed to be back here last night."

"That's not true!" Molly protested. "You had until sunup today, and you made it."

"I know, but that o'nery old hardhead wouldn't listen. He and I had some words, and we both ended up shouting mad."

Hildy swallowed hard, her hopes crushed.

"Oh, Joe," Molly whispered, "we needed that job so much. And the house. What about the house?"

"It's gone, too."

"Oh, Daddy," Hildy whispered. "You tried so hard."

Joe Corrigan rubbed his hand over his face and sighed deeply. "The old man was bad enough to talk to, but his son Don was worse. That's the meanest fourteen-year-old punk I ever met. He threatened to run me and my whole family clear out of the county."

"Whatever for?" Molly cried.

"Because I tried to reason with them, I guess. I tried to keep the job I was promised. I told them about driving day and night to get back on time."

Hildy's anger rose. "I'd like to meet up with them!" she exploded.

"No, you wouldn't, Hildy. The old man's got no more conscience than a rattler. And his son's cut out of the same cloth."

Molly sagged against her husband's chest, the sleeping baby unmindful of everything. "What'll we do, Joe?"

Hildy fought back tears. "Yes," she echoed softly, "what'll we do now?"

CHAPTER
SIX

TROUBLE COMES
RIDING

That Saturday morning in late June Hildy stood in shocked surprise beside her discouraged father and stepmother. Looking around the run-down tourist cabin grounds, she scuffed her bare feet in the dust.

So this is the Promised Land, she thought bitterly. *Millions of Americans out of work, and Daddy says that those few who do have jobs only earn an average of about seventeen dollars a week.* She swallowed hard. *And now my daddy has no job, no house, and no money. Our "forever home" is lost. Why, Lord?* her thoughts turned heavenward. *Daddy tried so hard. He deserved to have that job.*

For a moment, Hildy felt as she had when her mother died. God wasn't being fair. He certainly hadn't answered Hildy's prayers.

Then she remembered her recent change of heart and her grandmother's encouraging Bible verse about trusting in the Lord.

Hildy took a quick, deep breath. In all her twelve years,

whatever she had set her mind on she had been able to do. Months before, in the dark days following the death of their mother, Hildy had promised her younger sisters that they would have a home where they could stay forever. They would never have to move again.

Hildy had felt sure that was in California. Now the sudden loss of job and rental house was a setback. But there was no use worrying about the problem. She needed to set her mind on a solution.

"What're we going to do?" she again asked her father.

Hugging Molly and the baby closer to his chest, Joe Corrigan looked down at his daughter with a weak smile and slowly reached out his other arm to her. "We're a family," he said with a catch in his voice. "We'll work it out together." He gave her a big squeeze.

"But we're broke, Joe," his wife murmured softly. "We need food and shelter. We can't stay here. We're out of money."

He kissed her lightly on the forehead. "I'll try to trade some work for food—maybe sweep out a grocery store or something. I'll look for regular work, of course, and I'll try to find us some decent shelter. I know we don't have enough money even for one more night here."

Hildy forced herself to smile. "I'll help Molly with the kids while you find something. I know you can do it, Daddy."

Her father's face suddenly twisted, and bright tears glistened in his eyes. She hadn't seen him cry since her mother died shortly after Joey was born. "Thank—" Not able to finish what he started to say, he abruptly turned away. Walking rapidly to the Lexington Minuteman, he started it up and quickly drove away.

Molly and Hildy returned in silence to the cabin, where everyone except Ruby was still asleep.

Standing by the bed in her homemade flour sack underclothes, Ruby read the discouragement in their eyes. She started to speak, but Molly laid a warning finger across her lips and motioned the two girls to go outside.

Ruby slipped into her clothes and the two girls hurried out to the front stoop of the tourist cabin. When Hildy had explained the situation, Ruby doubled up her fists. "Makes me so fightin' mad I wanta smack them Gridleys clean into next week!"

Hildy looked out across the grounds at the other tourist cabins, and all she could see was poverty. The cabins were badly run down and needed repair. The few old cars sitting around under the sycamores were rusted junk piles. Three little boys, clad only in tattered shorts, were swinging in an old tire tied to a tree limb by a frayed rope. The kids were dirty and played silently without fun.

"No use fussing," Hildy replied. "My daddy'll find something. He always does."

"Yeah, but sometimes he drifted halfway acrost the whole United States a-doin' it!"

Hildy winced at the reference to her father's tendency to leave the family to look for work someplace else when things got tight. Before Hildy could answer, Molly opened the cabin door.

"Hildy, the baby needs milk, and the kids'll have to have something to eat when they wake up. Why don't you two girls go find a store?"

Hildy nodded and produced the coins her father had given her. Deciding that the main part of town was to their left, she started walking in that direction. "Come on, Ruby," she said. And her cousin joined her.

On the corner of the second block, they found a small grocery store with a single gasoline pump in front. Off to the right a boy who looked like he was slightly older than the girls was pumping up his bicycle's back tire with a red hose.

"Howdy," Ruby greeted him as the girls walked by. Hildy nodded and smiled at him. It was perfectly natural to be friendly back home in the Ozarks.

The boy glanced up. He was big with sandy-colored curly hair and dirty, work-hardened hands. Dropping the air hose, he stood up, scowling. "Howdeeee?" he mocked Ruby, drawing out the last syllable. "What kind of language is that?"

Hildy's whole being warned her not to answer but simply to enter the store.

But Ruby instantly exploded in hostility. "Why, that thar's friendly-like language," she replied sharply. "Like one civilized person speaks t'another. Not like dawgs that growl an' threaten!"

The big kid cocked his head, and he glared at Ruby with a hint of fire in his cold blue eyes. "You saying I'm not civilized?"

"I ain't a-sayin' what ye are, but y'all kin make of it what ye want!"

Hildy gripped Ruby's arm and tugged. "Come on," she whispered urgently. "Let's get the milk."

The boy's deeply tanned face broke into a crooked grin. "I make out you're both Okies or Arkies, fresh out of the backwoods."

Ruby stiffened and her fists came up defensively. "We'uns air from the Ozarks and mighty proud of it! Ye want to make somethin' out of it?"

The big kid's face clouded with anger; then he managed a faint smile. "I don't hit girls, not even if they're hillbillies."

Ruby took a menacing step toward the boy. "Hillbillies?" she snapped. "What's that? Somethin' nasty and low down?"

The boy threw back his head and laughed. "Whoever thought a person could be so dumb that they don't even know what a hillbilly is?"

"Take that back!" Ruby yelled.

Hildy grabbed her cousin's hand and pulled hard. "Please, Ruby. Let's go inside."

The teenage boy picked up his bicycle and threw his leg over the frame to settle on the seat. "That's good advice, Hillbilly Ruby."

Ruby jerked free of Hildy's grasp and started after the boy.

He pedaled off quickly but turned to call over his shoulder. "You two stay out of my way, or I'm liable to forget about not socking girls!"

Ruby ran after the boy, shouting and shaking her fists, but he just laughed.

Hildy trotted up to her cousin, gripped her arm firmly and led her into the tiny store.

A tired-faced old woman dressed in a poke bonnet and a long, frayed gingham dress came out of the back room in answer to the little bell that tinkled as the girls opened the door.

"'Morning, girls," she said without smiling. The lines in her face indicated her resignation to life, but discouragement plowed deep in every furrow. "What'll it be?"

Hildy spoke up immediately, hoping to get what they needed and hurry back to the cabin before they had any more trouble. "A loaf of light bread, twenty cents worth of baloney, and a bottle of milk," she said.

As the woman turned to fill the order, Ruby muttered under her breath about the boy on the bicycle.

Hildy glanced around the store. Everything was obviously hand built except for the small refrigerated unit. Even the shelves holding bread, canned goods, and other merchandise were roughly made.

In a few minutes the woman set the glass bottle of milk with the cream in the neck on the linoleum-covered counter. Next to it she placed a loaf of bread and a small package of bologna wrapped in brown butcher paper. "Thu'ty cents," she said.

Hildy counted out the coins on the woman's outstretched palm. "Thank you," she said, picking up the groceries with a smile.

As the girls started to turn toward the door, Ruby stopped and reached for something beside the hand-cranked cash register. "This a map of things hyar'bouts?" she asked.

The woman dropped the coins into the bronze-colored register. "What? Oh, yes, in a way. 'Tis a map of California. Lone River is on it. That is, if you look close."

Ruby started opening the map. "How about Grizzly Gulch?"

"Seems to me I've heard of it," the woman replied. "'Tis a ghost town, I think. Not far from here. Up in the Mother Lode country." She looked up curiously. "Do you want the map? Keep it."

"Thankee kindly," Ruby replied, opening the map on the counter. "Kin ye point me in the gen'ral d'rection of this here Mother Lode?"

The woman pulled a pair of glasses from under the counter and adjusted them on her nose. The left temple piece was missing, so the glasses sat on an angle. Bending over the map, she soon pointed. "There 'tis. Grizzly Gulch. Perhaps an hour's ride from here in a good car."

Ruby picked up a flat carpenter's pencil that lay on the counter and marked the spot. Then Hildy fairly dragged her cousin from the store and into the morning sunlight.

"Hildy," Ruby said, whacking the folded map across her open palm, "I'm gonna git up to that thar ghost town place and look fer my pa!"

"How're you going to do that?"

"I don't know yet, but I'm gonna do it. Ye kin bet yore bottom dollar on that."

Back at the cabin, Hildy had barely turned the groceries over to her stepmother when her father pushed the door open. "Get packed," he called. "I got us a place to camp for a while."

Hildy's hopes started to soar, then quickly plunged as her father explained. "It's just a place on a riverbed, but it's free. I talked to another man who's already camped there with his family."

Within minutes the Lexington Minuteman was on its way. And as it cruised through the town of Lone River, Hildy dealt with mixed feelings. Her eyes skimmed the houses in the town. "All these houses are really old, aren't they, Daddy?" she asked, trying to take her mind off her fear of what lay ahead.

"I'd say so," her father replied. "Some of those square, two-story wooden houses were probably built before 1900. Most of the houses are modest, though. Less than a thousand square feet. And I hear they cost less than a thousand dollars to build.

"What about those?" Hildy pointed to a group of large, elegant homes overlooking the river.

Her dad laughed. "Those are more like three to five thousand square feet, I reckon. And they're not cheap."

Hildy hardly heard his answer. *One of those*, she told herself, *could be our "forever home."* She sat back as her father drove out of town and crossed the river on a rusted metal bridge. In less than two miles, the flat valley gave way to dry, brown foothills. These in turn surrendered to real mountains, the majestic Sierra Nevadas that peaked some ten thousand feet above sea level.

Hildy's disappointment returned when her father turned off the paved road onto a country lane of ruts and bumps. Grass grew in the middle of the roadway. Oil and grease from the underside of passing cars had rubbed off on the weeds so that they were stunted and ugly but still clung to life. Finally the car stopped beside a clump of willows and two scraggly cottonwood trees.

Hildy sat forward in alarm. "That's not a river, is it, Daddy? Looks more like a dry creek bed."

"Dry this time of year because it usually doesn't rain around here from about May to November," her father said. He waved to a tall, skinny man in faded blue overalls who came out of a dirty-gray tent. "This place is dry, and it's free, although I'll have to haul water to drink. It's free, Hildy. I'll git us a tent like the Hocketts'—that's them camped across the creek bed—soon as I can."

In the next few minutes, Joe Corrigan unloaded the car, gave brief instructions for what to do until he returned, then drove off to look for work and a tent.

Molly stood with the baby in her arms, slowly turning around, surveying the desolate site.

Hildy had been watching the man in overalls and his family as they stood outside their tent flap, staring openly at the new arrivals. Hildy figured there was a wife and nine boys and girls all as skinny as their father. The oldest girl seemed about Hildy's age.

Hildy turned her eyes away from the other family and followed Molly's gaze. The dry creek bed lay in a small ravine, or wash, about forty feet wide. As far as Hildy could see in any direction, some kind of grain stretched to the horizon. Hildy guessed the crop was wheat. It was turning from green to early summer brown. A hot, dry wind blew like a warning blast across Hildy's face.

Ten-year-old Elizabeth rushed to her stepmother and stomped her foot. "I hate this place!" she announced.

"Me, too!" Martha echoed.

Sarah sighed. "Hildy, this don't look like a 'forever home' to me."

Little Iola tugged on Molly's skirt. "Let's go back to the Ozarks!" she cried.

Hildy squatted beside her sisters to assure them that everything would turn out all right, but she was interrupted by a call.

"Hi!" The greeting came from the tent across the dry creek bed. "I'm Twyla. Twyla Hockett," said the girl. She was about Hildy's age, with gray eyes and brown, stringy hair. "I live in that tent." She pointed.

Hildy stood up. "Oh, hi. I'm Hildy Corrigan. That's my stepmother, Molly, my cousin Ruby Konning, and my kid sisters: Elizabeth, Martha, Sarah, and Iola. The baby's Joey."

"Right proud to make yore acquaintance, I'm shore," Twyla said, crossing the creek bed to meet them. "My folks'll likely come a-callin' soon, but Mom says it hain't polite to go visitin' new neighbors without you bring salt and bread fer a gift. Raht now, we're a mite short of vittles."

While Hildy was trying to guess where the girl was from, she looked up to see a horse topping a rise above the ravine.

The rider stood up in the stirrups and shaded his eyes with his hands. "Hey, you Okies! What are you doing on my property?"

Just then the skinny man in overalls came out of his tent, and Hildy felt sure he was Twyla's father.

Ruby came to Hildy's side. "Ain't that thar guy on horseback the same smart-mouthed kid we seen at the little store in town?" she whispered.

As the rider got closer and dismounted, Hildy nodded. "That's the same one, all right."

The boy removed his sweat-stained cowboy hat and waved it at everyone. "Get off of this ranch!" he shouted. "We don't allow no Okies or Arkies polluting the place where our cattle graze."

Ruby took two quick steps and faced the boy. "Now lookee here, kid. Who d'you think ye are, a-bustin' in here orderin' decent folks 'round?"

The boy stood by the horse's head, reins in his hands, studying Ruby. A slow grin broke across his face. "I know you. You're Hillbilly Ruby."

"Don't ye go a-callin' me no names. Take that back, raht now!"

"Who's going to make me?"

Hildy reached for Ruby's hand, but it was too late. Ruby struck out fast like a snake's head. Knocking the boy's high-crowned cowboy hat off, she grabbed a handful of sandy-colored hair.

"Ouch!" the kid yelled. "Let go!"

"Not 'less'n ye say uncle!"

The boy tried to swing, but his arms were too short, and Ruby held him at arms' length. Anyone who didn't recognize the girl's anger and physical strength before would now be a believer.

The boy let out a yell. "You let go or my father will have you all in jail!" he threatened.

"Well, now," Ruby said through a smile that held no joy, "ye jist better 'polagize to us fer callin' names, or I'm plumb gonna snatch ye bald-headed this very instant."

Hildy tried again. "Ruby, please don't make things worse."

Ruby ignored her cousin. "Ye want yore hair tore out in chunks er one-by-one?" She started backing away, still gripping his hair.

Dropping the horse's reins, the boy went with Ruby, head slightly bowed to ease the pain of her grip.

Again Hildy started to tell Ruby to let the kid go.

Just then Twyla ran up and whispered in Hildy's ear. "That there's Don Gridley she's leadin' 'round like a puppy dog," she said. "Ever hear of the Gridleys?"

Hildy nodded and turned frightened eyes on the new girl. "This is *his* property? You sure?"

"Positive!"

Hildy hurried to Ruby and whispered the terrible news.

Ruby looked at her cousin and mouthed, "The boss's son?"

Hildy nodded, her mouth dry.

Ruby paused a moment, then released the boy's hair. "Since ye prob'bly got work to do afore yore pa whales the tar outta ye, I'll let ye go," she said in mock confidence. "But don't ye never smart off aroun' me er my friends agin, hear?"

The boy in cowboy boots and blue jeans straightened up, seething in anger and glowering at Ruby. He seemed about to say something, but then he turned, ran to the horse, caught up the reins, and leaped into the saddle.

"Every one of you better be off this property by sunup to-morrow," he yelled with a deep scowl, "or you'll all be in big trouble!" Savagely jerking the horse's head around, he raced away, boot heels drumming on the gelding's flanks.

Hildy watched him go, then turned to Ruby. "Now what've we done?"

CHAPTER SEVEN

A NEW FRIEND

After that initial excitement, the rest of the day dragged on. Hildy and Ruby helped Molly make rough beds of old quilts under the sparse shade of the willows and cottonwoods so that the baby and Iola could nap. Hildy and her cousin sat by the sleeping children, taking turns waving an old tea towel to keep insects away.

Elizabeth and Martha approached Hildy and sat down beside her. "I don't like this place," Martha complained. "It's hot. And the mosquitoes and flies are terrible, too."

"You promised us a 'forever home,'" Elizabeth reminded her. "This is worse than the sharecropper cabins we lived in."

Hildy reached out and hugged both sisters close. "It'll work out. You'll see."

"When?" asked Elizabeth, who was always practical.

"Shhh!" Ruby warned. "Here come the new neighbors. Ye want them to hear ye complainin'?"

The girls didn't reply. Hildy and Ruby turned to meet the Hocketts. The whole family had come—father, mother, and a whole raft of kids behind Twyla. All the kids had very skinny arms and legs, but their stomachs stuck out.

Molly frowned and walked toward them, whispering to herself, "They're starving, poor things."

Ruby stood up beside Molly. "What makes ye say that?"

"Stomachs sticking out like that from skinny bodies mean malnutrition," Molly replied softly.

Hildy wanted to whip out Spud's dictionary to look up the word *malnutrition*, but the Hocketts were too close.

"Howdy do, Missus," the other woman said from deep within her faded calico poke bonnet. "We be the Hocketts. I'm Zelda. My husbun's Bate, and these are our young'uns."

She pointed at the children. "That's Burl. He's fifteen. Twyla is thirteen, Ferris is past eleven, and Charley's barely ten. Alvira over there is eight, Mattie's six, Abner's four, and Inez is two and a half. The baby—she's named Kallie—is eleven months."

Hildy couldn't remember any name except Twyla's, but she counted nine Hockett kids—five girls and four boys.

"Hello, Miz' Hockett, Mr. Hockett," Molly acknowledged with a bob of her head. "This's my stepdaughter Hildy and her cousin, Ruby. That's Elizabeth, and this one's Martha. The rest of the kids is napping. My husband's looking for work."

Mr. Hockett spoke for the first time. "I purely do hope he has better luck'n I've had." His voice was soft and sad.

Mrs. Hockett held out a small package to Molly. "Me'n Bate want to welcome y'all as neighbors. Here's some salt and a bit of homemade bread. Salt fer keepin' our friendship long an' bread fer the staff o' life, ye know."

Hildy didn't know what Mrs. Hockett was talking about, but Molly seemed to understand.

"Much obliged," Molly said, accepting the hospitality gifts. "Come over under the shade and sit a spell."

"Don't mind if I do," replied Mrs. Hockett.

Mr. Hockett said very little, and Hildy had a feeling he was so far down on his luck that he didn't feel like talking or visiting. Even so, Hildy realized that tradition must have demanded that the Hocketts welcome the new family with a food gift.

As the Hocketts sat down in the cottonwoods' shade, Molly smiled at Mrs. Hockett. "We just got in today, so I'm ashamed to say I haven't had time to bake yet. But if you'll forgive my manners, Hildy will serve you some store-bought light bread and baloney."

"Oh, boy!" the younger Hockett children cried together. "Baloney san'wiches!"

Their mother and father gave them warning looks, which Molly pretended not to notice. She motioned Hildy to bring the meager food supply which the girls had purchased that morning in Lone River. Hildy wondered what her family would eat for supper, but she knew that Molly sincerely meant to share her food with the Hocketts.

When Hildy returned with the bread and sliced meat, Molly took the food and smiled at her stepdaughter. "Hildy, after our company's had a bite, why don't you older girls take our new neighbor kids over into that field and play fox and geese or burn base?"

"Yes'm," Hildy answered, moving over next to Twyla. The two girls smiled at each other.

After the kids had gobbled down the bread and meat, Ruby started playing fox and geese with them. Hildy and Twyla were already enjoying talking so much that they didn't join in the game. Instead they walked along the dry creek bed and told each other about themselves.

In some special, mysterious way, Hildy and Twyla instantly became friends.

As Twyla reached out to snap a twig off the end of a willow, Hildy glanced at her new friend's rough-looking hands. "You ever pick cotton?" she asked.

"Did I!" Twyla exclaimed. Popping the willow twig into her mouth, she held up her hands, palms forward. "How d'ye reckon I got these so tore up?"

"Me, too," Hildy replied, extending her hands. "In the Texas Panhandle."

"Same here." Twyla gently rubbed her damaged hands. "Got

paid thu'ty cents fer a hunnert-pound sack. No gloves nor nothing fer my knees." She pulled up her long, blue cotton dress to
show Hildy her badly scarred knees.

Hildy grinned and did the same. "Hard to tell who's got the
worst-looking knees, huh?"

Twyla shook her head. "Pullin' off the bolls without gloves
was the worst," she said. "I reckon my hands never will heal
right. See?"

"Same here." Hildy turned her palms up. "I guess maybe
that's what made me decide to get an education, so I'd never
have to pick cotton again."

"An edjacation?" Twyla asked wistfully. "We hardly never
git to go to school 'cause we move 'round so much, an' Pop
needs all us kids to help work in the fruit and things."

"Fruit?"

"Picking fruit—apricots, and peaches, and such. That's
mostly what they grow in the valley around here." She paused
for a moment, thinking. "Well, they's cattle and some wheat in
the foothills. But we follow the fruit. Guess that's why local folks
call us fruit tramps." She turned sad gray eyes upon Hildy and
asked, "What grade are ye in?"

"Eighth."

"How old are ye?"

"Twelve."

"I'm thirteen, but I'm only in the fifth, that is, when I kin go
to school a'tall."

Soon the conversation turned to Don Gridley's warning
about getting off the property. Hildy frowned with concern.
"What can he do if we don't leave?"

Twyla shrugged. "I'm skeered to think. Git us fer trespassin',
I s'pose, maybe more. My pop worked for him once, but Don
lied and got Pop in trouble. Don claimed Pop set fire to a wheat
field, but Pop thinks Don done it a-purpose jist to blame my
pop. Don's a mean one!"

Hildy picked up a small stone from the dry creek bed and
idly tossed it into the air and caught it again. She had already

formed her own opinion of Don Gridley, but she asked, "How so?"

"We been here since Easter, so we've seen enough of that there Gridley boy to know he's sorta strange. My pop says he's not right in the head, says he's been called a pyromaniac or somethin'."

Hildy started to ask what that was, then decided she'd wait and look it up in Spud's dictionary when she got back to camp.

"Don purely hates all us po' folks," Twyla added. "Says we should all be sent back where we came from or be burned out."

"Burned out?"

"Our tent, I guess. The good Lord knows we ain't got much else to burn."

"Maybe he was just bluffing," Hildy suggested.

"Maybe, but jist the same, I wisht yore cousin hadn't riled him up, a-leadin' him 'round by his hair like she done."

The girls' conversation drifted on to more pleasant subjects, and by the time they returned to the camp, a strong bond of friendship had formed between them.

That night, Hildy helped her stepmother try to heat the last can of green beans for supper. But she found it very difficult to cook in a pan awkwardly balanced between two flat rocks over a small, smoky fire. No matter which way Hildy stood, the smoke blew into her face. Her eyes smarted and she coughed a lot, but eventually the meal was served.

Molly instructed the children to sit around in a circle well back from the fire. "Children," she began, "I know your father doesn't go in much for saying a blessing, but—"

Martha interrupted. "Our mother does." She paused, lowered her head and added softly, "Did."

The other sisters nodded.

"Then you'll understand what I was going to suggest," Molly continued. "Let's bow our heads and I'll ask the blessing."

Hildy was so surprised that she barely remembered to bow her head while Molly raised her voice slightly in prayer.

"Lord," Molly began, "we're mighty thankful that we

reached California safely. We're thankful we have something to eat, and even had a little to share with our new neighbors."

Hildy felt little Iola squirming beside her, and she patted her little sister on the leg.

"We're starting a new life here," Molly continued, "and we'd be mighty grateful if you would help us to live in peace and plenty. Help Joe to find a job—and help Mr. Hockett, too. We ask this in Jesus' name. Amen."

Hildy felt strangely stirred by her stepmother's simple prayer. Maybe Hildy wasn't the only one starting to trust the Lord again.

About an hour later, after the family had finished eating, Molly was lighting a coal oil lamp as her husband drove up in the Lexington Minuteman. A long pole and a roll of blue canvas stuck out in front and back of the car's top.

"Look!" Hildy cried, putting down the rag she'd been using to wash dishes. "He's got a tent! We won't have to sleep under the stars."

Outrunning her sisters, Hildy reached the car first. She jumped up on the running board and stuck her head inside the car to kiss her father on the cheek.

"Daddy, it's beautiful. But I never saw a blue tent before. Did you get a job?"

"No job." His voice was low and sad. "Traded one of the two spares for the tent."

Hildy blinked and drew back as her father's warm breath touched her face. "Daddy! You've been drinking!"

"Shhh! Molly and the kids'll hear you."

"You promised when Mom died, no more!" Hildy scolded.

"Help get the tent off the car and set up!" her father snapped.

Stung by the unexpected harshness in her father's voice, her temper flared. "We can't! We've got to be off this property by sunup," she said, briefly explaining about Don's warning.

Her father muttered angrily in frustration, then nodded. "I didn't know this was their land, too," he said. "We won't set up the tent then. It'll attract too much attention. We'll just sleep under the stars."

Hildy felt sick inside. Nothing was going right, but her father's drinking troubled her more than anything else. He never touched liquor unless he was very upset. Silently Hildy helped Molly get the kids to bed, wondering what was going to happen to them. When they were settled, she sat down on the ground by the lamp.

The yellow glow of the coal oil lamp placed on an upended lug box gave enough light to see but not much for reading. Still, Hildy took out the Bible her grandfather had given her and strained her eyes as she began to read. She had decided to read her Bible every night, but on a trip like this, it wasn't always easy. After reading a chapter from the New Testament, she put the Bible away and picked up Spud's dictionary.

Opening the small, well-worn book, she looked up the words she had heard that day.

Malnutrition: lack of proper nourishment. That made sense.

Pyromaniac: one with a compulsion to set things on fire. Then she had to look up the word *compulsion*.

Compulsion: a strong, irresistible impulse.

Hildy sighed, then forced her thoughts from the Hocketts and Don Gridley to Spud. *Wish I could see Spud again sometime*, she thought.

About that time, Molly spread some more old blankets, quilts, and coats on the ground for bedding. Soon the lamp was blown out, and Hildy stared up into the shimmering stars in the ink-black sky overhead.

In the silence of the night, Molly's voice came in a whisper. "Why, Joe?" she asked, but he did not answer.

Hildy knew her father wouldn't be able to hide the liquor on his breath from Molly.

Before long, everyone slept except Hildy. Her anger burned against Don Gridley and his father for the terrible things happening to the Corrigans, especially Hildy's father.

I wish the Gridleys knew what it's like, she thought, *not having*

any food, or money, or job, or decent place to live! Hildy promptly
scolded herself. She raised her eyes in the darkness. "Sorry,
Lord," she whispered. "I didn't mean that. I wouldn't wish this
kind of life on anybody."

But in a way, she did mean it. And that troubled her as she
waited for sleep, which was a long time in coming.

The next morning, the Corrigans and the Hocketts hurried
to move out before Don Gridley came by. The two fathers
weren't afraid of the boss's son, but they knew that Mr. Gridley
was the richest man in the county, and he might support his
son by having the two men jailed for trespassing.

Hildy watched the Hocketts stack all their mattresses and the
tent on top of their Studebaker. She turned to her father. "Where
we going now, Daddy?"

"I don't know. We'll have to look for a place."

Again Hildy felt a terrible lack of "roots" as she said goodbye
to Twyla. Then the two families got into their cars, and Mr.
Hockett started off first with the mattresses flopping up and
down on the roof, making the car top-heavy.

Hildy sighed and waved to Twyla. *I wonder if I'll ever see her
again*, Hildy wondered.

CHAPTER EIGHT

SEARCH IN A GHOST TOWN

J ust as Hildy wondered if she'd ever again see her new friend, Twyla, Mr. Hockett stuck his hand out of the old Studebaker and motioned for Mr. Corrigan to stop.

Hildy leaned forward as her father eased his Lexington Minuteman up alongside the Hocketts' vehicle with its top load of mattresses.

Twyla's father waved. "Joe, I just thought of a place I saw when I was fishin'!" he cried. "Be a good place to camp. Follow me."

Hildy's father nodded and let the Studebaker pull ahead again. Then they turned off the main paved highway leading from the foothills into Lone River. In a few minutes Mr. Hockett pulled off the paved road onto a large area of sand and rocks. This cut through the sandy bank toward the stream that gave the nearby community of Lone River its name.

"What's he doin'?" Ruby asked anxiously as Mr. Hockett

carefully eased his old car down the western shore into the shallow stream.

Hildy leaned out the window and gazed at the riffling hundred-foot-wide river with large stones on the bottom.

"Must be shallow enough to cross," Hildy's father said, following the Studebaker into the water. "Hang on, everybody. We're going to do the same."

Little Iola bounced up and down on the seat. "Look out, Daddy!" she cried. "You'll drown the car and us, too!"

He laughed. "Don't worry, honey. We won't drown," he assured her.

Hildy's sisters and Ruby stuck their heads out of the car to see how deep the water really was. The stream didn't quite reach the hub caps and ran below the wide running boards.

Hildy glanced up as the Hockett car lurched and seemed about to tip over with the weight of the mattresses on top. Then the Studebaker righted itself and crawled out of the river on the far shore.

A moment later Hildy's father drove up alongside the Studebaker, and they parked in the shade of an ancient two-hundred-foot-long bridge with iron trestles.

Hildy grinned at Twyla next to her in the Studebaker. "We meet again."

"Yeah, and this time I hope that mean ol' Don Gridley don't bother us none."

The girls' fathers got out of their cars to discuss where each would pitch the family tent.

Twyla's father scratched his head. "I cain't sleep all of my kids inside, so some have to sleep out. We all got mattresses, but since y'all ain't got none, I'll he'p ye cut some green boughs from willows and them cottonwoods. They got spring in 'em, so they'll make a tolerable mattress. Throw some old blankets or coats on them, and yore family'll have passable beddin'."

"Much obliged," Hildy's father replied.

As the men started unloading the cars, Hildy's stepmother glanced nervously at the river. "Joe," she whispered. "We're surely not going to stay here."

"For a while, we are."

"But the river's so close. The children are so small, and not one of them can swim."

"It's shallow, Molly."

"But there might be deep holes or sudden drop-offs, Joe."

"It'll only be for a little while. You'll just have to keep an extra close eye on the kids until I can find us a better place."

Hildy came close. "Ruby and I'll help," she offered. "We won't let anything happen."

Molly looked doubtful. "I'm sure you'll be very careful, but a river can be so treacherous."

Hildy studied the area. The stream flowed swiftly through the bottom of a small ravine with high sides. Close by, it was shallow and pleasant to see and hear. But a hundred yards downstream, the water was swift, dark, and deep. On both banks, rustling cottonwood trees stood like green sentinels. Smaller willows bent over the water between the taller trees.

Hildy sniffed. "What's that funny smell?"

Mr. Hockett walked over to his car to get another load for the tent. "Eucalyptus trees," he replied. "Early settlers planted 'em over yonder. Cain't see 'em from here, but ye kin sure smell 'em. Kinda stinky like."

Ruby wrinkled her nose. "They shore are," she agreed.

Mr. Hockett pointed to the river. "Downstream, past where we crossed, they's some deep holes. Lotsa big cats and some carp. Make good eatin'."

"Uhh!" Iola exclaimed. "Who wants to eat cats?"

Twyla smiled. "My pop means catfish, honey."

Mr. Hockett continued. "In the winter, these shallows will be so filled with salmon goin' upstream to spawn that ye kin almost walk on 'em."

"I've read about them!" Hildy cried. "They're big fish that live in the sea. How do they get way back up here in this river?"

Twyla's father leaned against the Studebaker. "They come in from the Pacific Ocean to San Francisco Bay," he explained. "Then they foller the San Joaquin River upstream to where it meets Lone River."

Twyla moved close to Hildy. "He spears them salmon so we kin eat," she whispered. "They're as long as you are tall, sometimes."

Joe Corrigan returned to the Minuteman car. "I'll bring all of you kids back here next winter so you can see for your-selves," he promised.

Hildy took a quick, short breath. Did that mean her father wasn't going to move away as he always did when he didn't have a job? Hildy was afraid to ask, but she dared to hope that this time the family really would stay put. And eventu-ally they would find their "forever home."

In an hour, both families had set up camp about a hundred feet apart in the shadow of the bridge. A few cars and a couple teams of horses clattered over. Otherwise, the area was quiet and peaceful with only the sound of the river flow-ing over the stones.

When the boughs had been cut for mattresses and crude fire pits made of river stones, the men drove off, looking for work.

After Molly was satisfied that the family's few possessions were placed in the best possible places in the tent, Hildy and Ruby went outside to talk with Twyla. Molly and Mrs. Hock-ett told the girls they would watch the other children so the three older girls could go for a walk.

Hildy, Ruby, and Twyla walked downstream past where the cars had crossed. Hildy and Twyla began talking and laughing as though they had known each other all their lives. Ruby joined in for a few minutes, then fell into silence, star-ing into space. Finally she sat down with her feet almost in the water.

Twyla looked at Hildy. "Did I say somethin' wrong?" she asked anxiously.

"No, no. She's just thinking. You see, she recently found out that her father may be living in California. She's never seen him and her mother's dead. So Ruby's hoping to find her dad out here."

"I'm right sorry fer her," Twyla said with concern. "I'm glad I got me a daddy, even if'n it's pow'rful hard for him to get a job and hold it."

"How long's he been out of work?"

"Cain't rightly say. Long time." Twyla lowered her voice and glanced around. "It's been mighty slim pickin's 'round our place fer too long, though. 'Course, it ain't Pop's fault. He's got a bum back and cain't hardly work a full day without it hurtin' him somethin' awful."

The two girls walked on, sharing secrets as only close friends can.

Hildy sighed. "I sure hope my daddy finds work soon. Otherwise, I'm afraid he'll take off for Oregon, or Texas, or someplace and leave us behind again while he looks for work. He's done that lots of times."

"Pop's never gone off like that," Twyla mused, "but he don't hardly work much a'tall no more. 'Course, like I said, it ain't really his fault."

The girls kept walking until they came to a barbed-wire fence. There a hand-lettered sign on a post read "Keep Out!"

"Guess we better turn back," Hildy said. "I see Ruby's already done that."

Back at the camp, Ruby ran off to play with the younger kids.

Twyla stopped and faced her new friend. "Y'know somethin', Hildy?" she said. "Life's been so grim so long it's plumb good to have someone like you to talk to. I feel like we've been best friends forever and ever."

"Me, too," Hildy agreed.

In the early afternoon, Hildy's father returned across the river. For a moment, Hildy was afraid to come close, fearful she would again smell alcohol on his breath. But when he got out of the car with a big grin, Hildy knew he had good news.

"Got a lead on a job!" he announced loudly, scooping his younger daughters into his arms.

As the family came whooping happily around, Joe Corrigan turned to look soberly at Ruby. "It's in a place called . . . Grizzly Gulch!"

Ruby sucked in her breath sharply. "Ye mean . . . where my father might be workin'?"

"Yep. Now, don't get your hopes up too high, but if you want to ride along—"

"When do we start?" Ruby interrupted.

The Hocketts, hearing the Corrigans' joyful shouts, came over to see what was going on. When it was explained, Mrs. Hockett and Twyla volunteered to help Molly with the kids so Hildy could ride along with her father and Ruby.

Within minutes the Lexington Minuteman turned east, away from Lone River, and climbed into the foothills of California's Mother Lode country. Ruby was too excited to talk, but Hildy chattered endlessly.

"This is near where James Marshall discovered gold in 1848 and set off the famous Gold Rush of '49," she said. "I read about that back in the Ozarks, but I never dreamed I'd see this country."

Grizzly Gulch lived up to its reputation of being a ghost town. The Great Depression had hit hard. The price of gold had dropped to about thirty dollars an ounce, Mr. Corrigan explained. Almost everybody had moved away. The streets were largely deserted.

Smelly trees called Chinese trees of heaven grew in scraggly clumps in alleys, in sidewalk cracks, and against every vacant building.

Hildy surveyed the area doubtfully. "Doesn't look like much work here, Daddy."

"Can't leave any stone unturned," he replied, steering the touring car under the shade of a wide-leafed catalpa tree.

"Well, there's the place I was told to apply."

A small bell mounted over the door sounded as the three walked into a tiny cafe. An old woman in a flowered apron was pushing pine-scented sawdust across the floor with a worn-out broom.

Mr. Corrigan cleared his throat. "Mrs. Titus?"

"She ain't here. I'm her maw. What kin I do fer ye?"

"I was told there might be a job here . . . uh . . . washing dishes."

"Mister, there ain't no job in this town for a growed man. Not even washin' dishes."

Hildy swallowed her disappointment as her father hesitated. She watched the hope drain from his eyes. He was a proud man in his own way, and washing dishes wasn't something she ever thought he would consider.

Ruby stepped forward. "Ye know a man named Konning?"

The old woman's aged-lined face seemed to soften a moment. "Highpockets Konning?"

Ruby reached out and grabbed the old woman's hands where they gripped the broom handle. "Where is he?" she asked excitedly.

"Gimme back my broom!" the old woman growled, shaking off Ruby's eager hands. She cocked a suspicious eye on Ruby. "What d'ye want him fer?"

"He's . . . he's my . . . pa."

The old woman started to speak, then broke into a grin before throwing back her head to laugh loudly. "I don't know who ye really are, li'l gal, but you ain't no kin of Highpockets. No sireee!"

Deep disappointment clouded Ruby's eyes.

Hildy spoke up. "What makes you say that?" she asked.

The woman's watery blue eyes focused on Hildy with a sharpness that seemed to go right through her. "Because Highpockets worked here'bouts fer years afore he moved on, and many a time I've heard him say he didn't have no chick ner kin."

Ruby started to turn away, then spun back. "Did he ever say anythin' 'bout bein' married?"

"Well, now that ye mention it, yes. I rec'lect his wife died when they was both young. But he didn't have no kids."

"Maybe," Ruby continued, "he didn't know he had no daughter. Maybe he heerd his wife died, but nobody tol' him she had a little girl jist afore she passed on."

The woman's eyes narrowed thoughtfully. "Tell ye what," she said, leaning the broom against a red brick wall. "Why don't we all sit down and talk a spell? Maybe I kin he'p ye find Highpockets."

An hour later, Mr. Corrigan reluctantly agreed to let Ruby stay at the cafe, working for room and board for a week or so while she looked for her father.

Hildy couldn't help but wonder if her father was a little relieved to have one less mouth to feed, but it was hard for Hildy to say goodbye to her cousin. "I hope you find him, Ruby," she said, swallowing with difficulty.

"You're not saying goodbye forever," her father assured the girls. "We'll see you soon, Ruby."

On the drive back toward the valley, Hildy voiced her worst fears. "Daddy, if you can't find work around here, are you going to leave us and look someplace else, like before?"

"Maybe this place isn't right for us, Hildy. I mean, with old man Gridley firing me, and camping by that river where a kid could drown. So if I don't find something here pretty soon, maybe I'll look in Oregon. I hear they need men in the timber there."

Now Hildy felt even more frightened. She gulped. "Would you take us with you?" she asked.

"It'd be better if you stayed here. I'll send for you and the rest of the family when I find work."

Hot tears of frustration sprang to Hildy's eyes. She blinked very fast. Nothing was going right in California. Yet she had been so sure things would be different here.

As the car passed through a small town, Mr. Corrigan began looking around. "See if you can spot a liquor store, Hildy," he said.

She spun angrily toward him. "Daddy!"

"Don't preach to me, Hildy."

"Oh, Daddy! Please don't!"

He slammed his open palm on the steering wheel, and Hildy slumped in the seat. She understood her father's frustration but not his occasional weakness to drink.

I wish Ruby were here to talk to, she told herself, *. . . or Spud.* That thought surprised her. She shook the name out of her mind.

The rest of the trip passed in silence. By the time they reached camp again, Hildy had one thing to be glad about. Her father had not stopped along the way for liquor.

Hildy raised her eyes and uttered a silent prayer. *Thanks, Lord, but something's got to happen soon, or nothing'll stop Daddy. We need some hope fast—before it's too late!*

CHAPTER NINE

TROUBLE AT A BRUSH ARBOR

At dawn the following Sunday, Hildy opened her eyes to the sight of the blue tent overhead. The old tent smelled dusty. But that odor mixed with the sweet, clean fragrance of cottonwoods and willows, and there was just a hint of the pungent odor from the distant eucalyptus trees. The river had a smell, too. Hildy couldn't decide whether she liked it or not.

She sat up on her pallet of old quilts spread over springy willow and cottonwood boughs. This was a long way from the "forever home" she had thought awaited them in California. The camp was not even safe. The river posed a constant danger to both the Corrigan and the Hockett children.

We have to get a home of our own, Hildy thought, swinging her legs off the bedding. Her pallet lay against the back of the tent close to the right wall. Hildy would have to share the pallet when Ruby returned. Elizabeth and Martha slept on similar bedding at Hildy's feet. The two younger sisters slept along the left wall. Hildy's father and stepmother had already gotten up from their pallet by the tent flap, and Hildy could hear Molly feeding the baby.

Every inch of space, except a narrow dirt walkway from the tent opening to the beds, was filled with pots, pans, eating utensils, clothing, and personal items. These spilled over onto the front wall of the tent.

A flap covered the single opening in the middle of the tent front. There were no windows, so the flap had been left open the night before, and the two side walls had been propped up with boxes to permit some of the late June night breeze to enter the sweltering tent.

Hildy pulled on her clothes but not her shoes. She usually went barefoot from April to September. Quietly crawling to the flap, careful not to wake her sisters, she peered through the tent flap. Her father was squatting on the ground, building a fire in the stone pit.

Hildy stood up, her unbraided, long hair falling everywhere about her shoulders. She studied her father with concern. He looked tired, as though he hadn't slept well. Walking over to him, she patted him on the back reassuringly. "Daddy, you'll find a job," she said. "I know you will."

"Thanks." He stood up and putting his arm around her thin shoulders, he gently stroked her uncombed hair. "Soon's I do, we'll find a house and move away from here." He glanced up toward the other tent. "Oh, there's your new friend. She's motioning for you to come over. Go ahead, but don't be gone long."

As the two girls approached each other, grinning in happy greeting, Twyla spoke first. "Wanna take a walk?" she asked.

"Sure. Just so we stay close so I can help with breakfast or the kids when they wake up."

"Ye wanna watch my father work his trotlines?"

"What's that?"

Twyla explained as the girls walked downstream along the sandy riverbank. " 'Stedda fishin' with one pole like most folks, last night Pop baited a whole buncha hooks and strung 'em from one long line. He tied one end to that cottonwood thar in front of us. See it?"

Hildy nodded.

"Then Pop waded across the shallows with the rest of them hooks and the line," Twyla continued. "He tied t'other end to that willer tree. See it?"

"Yes."

"Then he let the baited hooks down at the edge o' the rapids. The current carried them hooks over the end of the falls into a big hole. See there by that big ol' snag? They's a deep drop-off that runs from there halfway across the river. Lotsa good-sized catfish on the bottom. Sometimes Pop brings home a whole gunnysack full of 'em."

The girls approached as Mr. Hockett waded into the hip-deep water at the downstream side of the rapids. He started pulling in the hooks at the far shore.

"See there? He uses bread dough balls wrapped in teeny pieces of old cloth so the bait won't fall off the hook," Twyla explained. It's also harder fer fish to steal bait thata way. Still, ye kin see they've stripped the bait from the first two hooks. Maybe he'll have better luck on the next one."

He did. The girls cheered as Mr. Hockett pulled up a large, wiggling catfish. Its dark-colored back glistened in contrast to its whitish underside.

Mr. Hockett called to the girls. "About two pounds, I'd say!"

Twyla nudged Hildy. "Watch how he takes the fish off carefully, hand in front of the back fin so's it cain't stick Pop. See? Now he'll drop that fish in the gunnysack tied to his belt," she explained. "By the time he finishes checkin' all the hooks, we'll have enough to give yore folks some. Ye like catfish?"

Hildy didn't care for it, but she didn't want to offend her new-found friend. "If it's cooked right," she said.

"My mama fries the best catfish anywhere," Twyla remarked proudly. "Jist ye wait and see. Well, come on. Let's walk some more."

After a few minutes they came again to the barbed-wire fence with its "Keep Out!" sign. Hildy's eyes followed the fence away from the river, and farther down she noticed another hand-lettered sign she hadn't seen before. "Keep Out! Gridley Ranches Will Prosecute Trespassers to the Full Extent of the Law!"

Hildy turned to Twyla. "Is this the same Gridley that fired our fathers?"

"Shore is. Richest man in the county, and the meanest. Well, 'less'n ye count his son Don. He's meaner'n a sackful o' wildcats."

Hildy glanced nervously around. A lone rider was making his way along the other side of the fence about a quarter mile away from the river.

"Is that Don?" Hildy asked.

"Too far away to say fer shore."

"Well, let's not stay here and find out. We've got enough troubles without running into him again."

By the time the girls returned to camp, the two fathers had skinned the fish. Both outdoor fires had been built up with stones so that each blaze burned hotly under large cast-iron skillets.

"Ummm!" Hildy exclaimed. "That smells good. I never thought I'd love the fragrance of catfish for breakfast."

"Wait'll ye get really hongry," Twyla said with a halfhearted smile. "Then ye'll want to eat the skins, too."

Just then Molly stuck her head out of the tent. "Hildy," she called, "the girls are up. Please take them down to the river and help them wash. And be careful, please. That current's swift."

"Guess I'll do the same with my brothers and sisters," Twyla decided.

At the river, Hildy sat on a large boulder and braided her hair while her sisters cleaned up. None of them had toothbrushes. Neither did the Hockett kids. The Hocketts used salt on their forefingers to clean their teeth, and the Corrigan kids used baking powder.

When they had finished, all the younger children ran back toward the tents, laughing and chasing each other. Hildy followed, tying a white string at the end of each of her two braids.

The two families separated to eat at makeshift tables of boards set across large rocks.

Although Hildy was reluctant to try it at first, she found that fried catfish was delicious, even for breakfast.

Later, as Hildy was doing dishes in water that had been heated over the open fire, she caught a flash of light in the distance. She glanced toward the fence with its posted warning. Sunlight reflected off a boy's belt buckle.

"It's him!" she whispered.

Elizabeth, who was taking her turn to dry the dishes, looked at Hildy oddly. "Huh?"

Hildy didn't want to alarm her sister, but she knew that Don Gridley was sitting on his horse, watching them. Hildy shrugged. "It's nothing. Here. Dry this one and we're done."

After Hildy had thrown out the dishwater, she went back to watching the younger children. Molly told her that she and Twyla's mother had decided to go into town with Hildy's father so that Mrs. Hockett could show Molly where to find the various stores. They were taking the younger kids with them, and Twyla's father was staying in camp to fix more trotlines.

As the Lexington Minuteman crossed the river, Hildy and Twyla discussed what they could do.

Hildy suddenly cocked her head. "Listen! I hear singing. Away off."

"Sounds like church," Twyla agreed.

"Church? Is it Sunday?"

"Reckon so." Twyla began moving her hand in time to the music. "Kinda purdy, ain't it?" She sang along softly, " 'Yes, we'll gather at the river, the beautiful, the beautiful river, gather with the saints at the river that flows by the throne of God.' "

Sudden, pleasant memories flooded over Hildy. She remembered attending a tiny Ozark church with her mother and singing that hymn Sunday after Sunday. She also remembered her recent recommitment to trust God. "Let's go see," she said.

Twyla looked down at her faded, tattered clothing. "We're not dressed fit fer church," she objected.

"We won't go in, just stand outside and listen."

The girls put on their only pair of shoes to walk across the hot rocks on the riverbed, then followed the singing away from the river and onto a small bluff overlooking the water. About a dozen tar-paper shacks and dirty white tents marked a small temporary community of migrant workers. At the edge of the settlement, there was a small open structure with a two-foot-tall cross of stained lath in the very center of the flat roof.

"A brush arbor!" Hildy exclaimed. "I haven't seen one of those for a long time."

"Lots of 'em 'round these parts," Twyla replied. "Mostly built by fruit tramps like us. People from Oklahoma, Arkansas, Texas, Missouri, and so forth, don't cotton much to the regular churches. That's why they make brush arbors."

As the girls approached, Hildy noticed that four posts about eight feet long had been sunk into the ground twenty feet or so apart. Branches from nearby peach, almond, and apricot orchards had been broken off and laid across the top as a roof. The hot sun had dried the leaves so they rustled lightly in the morning breeze. Only the lath cross stood firm.

In the shade below, about two dozen men and women in clean overalls and freshly ironed cotton dresses sang lustily. A young man with straight black hair falling over his eyes plucked a battered guitar to lead them as they sang.

The girls stopped at the back of the brush arbor, and Hildy leaned close to Twyla. "Makes you feel all warm and good inside, doesn't it?" she whispered.

Twyla nodded. "Shore does."

Hildy studied the rough benches—fifteen-foot cottonwood logs with the bark removed and two sides smoothed with an ax. One flat side rested in the dust churned up by passing feet. The other flat side served as a seat.

Hildy listened silently to the words of praise and promise in hymn after hymn. Each one was a little more spirited than the one before, a little louder and a little faster, and the people began clapping. Then an older woman jumped up, waving her hands and dancing in the dust with her eyes shut and her face up-turned.

Suddenly, from behind Hildy, someone laughed.

Startled, Hildy turned, too caught up in the happy music and hand clapping to have noticed anyone approaching.

Don Gridley and three other boys about his age had ridden up on horseback and dismounted. Each boy except Don dropped his reins so the horses stood ground-hitched. One boy was heavyset, another had red hair, and the third had a crooked nose, as though it had been broken and hadn't healed straight. All four wore cowboy hats, blue jeans, and clean work shirts.

"Well, now," Don said with a sneer as the singing broke off and everyone turned to face the back. "Lookee what we got here. A bunch of Okies and Arkies disturbing the peace."

The guitar player, resting the instrument on his knees, raised his head and spoke in a slow drawl from near the pulpit. "This hyar's the Lord's house, however temporary, so ever'body's welcome. C'mon in and take a seat, boys."

Don leaned forward and cupped his hand behind his ear. "I hear somebody speaking, but I didn't understand a word," he mocked. He turned to his three companions. "Any of you boys recognize that foreign language?"

The red-haired kid at Don's right put on a serious face. "I do believe these people are trying to speak English, but they can't be. We understand that language, but not theirs!"

Hildy stirred uneasily, not knowing what to do.

The movement caught Don's eyes, and he smiled without humor. "Hey, I know you. You're one of the Ozark gals." His eyes shifted to Twyla. "But you're not the blond hillbilly that yanked my hair." He turned back to Hildy. "Where is she? I owe her something."

Hildy tried to keep her voice steady. "Ruby's away."

"Ruby!" Don exclaimed, turning to his friends. "I remember now. Hillbilly Ruby. Fresh from the Ozarks. Well, I'll deal with her later. Right now, you—what's your name?"

"Hil . . . Hildy Corrigan. She's Twyla Hockett."

"Well, Hildy, you and Twyla got ten seconds to head back to the Ozarks. Me and my friends here are sworn to keep this county clean, and we're going to start by running all you Okies and Arkies out of the county."

Hildy stubbornly set her jaw. She swallowed hard, then shook her head.

Don dropped his horse's reins, reached into his tight blue jeans, and produced a small box of wooden matches. "Maybe we should start by burning this eyesore down."

Instantly, the worshipers started easing out of the shade produced by the dry tree boughs and leaves.

Hildy was surprised to hear her own voice, calm and strong, speaking up. "You're not going to do any such thing!"

Don stopped pulling matches from the box. "What did you say?"

Twyla tugged on Hildy's arm. "Let's git away whilst the gittin's good!"

Hildy pretended not to hear. "I said," she replied evenly, her eyes challenging Don's, "you're not going to burn this place."

"Who's going to stop me?" he sneered, striking a match with his dirty thumbnail.

Hildy hesitated, caught without an idea. At times like this she hated her impulsive nature. In sudden panic, she looked around, and her eyes rested on the four ground-hitched horses.

Without thinking, she reached out and grabbed the cowboy hat off the heavyset kid's head. He tried to stop her, but he was too slow.

Holding the hat by the brim, Hildy ran toward the horses. "Heyyyahhhh!" she yelled, waving the hat and slapping it down on Don's horse with a loud popping sound.

Whinnying, all four animals broke into a gallop across the open land toward the river.

"You dumb girl!" the heavyset kid cried, grabbing his hat from Hildy. "Look what you did."

"Shut up and catch them!" the red-haired boy yelled, running after the horses with the other two boys.

As the horses galloped away, they held their heads sideways so they wouldn't step on the trailing reins.

Don Gridley stood still, his eyes boring into Hildy. "You did it to me again, didn't you? Well, I'll get even." He turned and dashed after his friends.

Hildy felt a gentle hand on her arm. She turned to see the guitar player looking down at her.

"Miss, we'd be proud to make your acquaintance," he said. "And yore friend's."

Hildy tried to smile but couldn't. She knew that Don Gridley was going to make her life miserable. The question was *when* and *how*.

CHAPTER
TEN
———
WORD FROM SPUD

On the way back to the tents, Twyla began to laugh. "Ye shore showed *them*, Hildy!"

Hildy didn't feel like laughing. "I didn't know what else to do. Besides, I didn't think. I just acted. I've done that before. Always got me into trouble, and this time'll probably be the same."

Twyla grew serious, showing concern. "Ye reckon he'll really try to git even?"

"I'm sure of it. He scares me. I just hope he doesn't hurt my family."

"Pop says the Gridleys are all-pow'rful. When Mr. Gridley fired him, it weren't Pop's fault. It was really Don's. But Mr. Gridley said he'd see to it my pop won't never work agin in this here county. He even threatened to run Pop outta the county. So far, we're still here, but ain't nobody that'll hire Pop. He's pow'rful discouraged."

Hildy led the way down the sandy embankment by the river. "Couldn't he look someplace else?" she asked over her shoulder.

"No money for gasoline to git anywheres." Twyla slid down

the embankment to stand beside Hildy. "Things are gittin' mighty desper't at our tent."

Hildy hesitated to ask what Twyla meant. Instead she changed the subject back to the Gridleys. "I'm never again going to be considered inferior, like Don Gridley and his friends think I am!" she declared.

Twyla kicked at a river stone. "Ain't no way out fer us po' folks, ye know."

Hildy turned and grabbed her friend's shoulders hard. "Oh yes there is!" she exclaimed. "First, you've got to make up your mind what you want. Of course, you've got to be sure that's what God wants for you, too, but then you have to go after it and never quit."

Twyla gently pulled loose from Hildy's firm grip. "Maybe they's a way fer you, Hildy, but not fer me."

"Yes, there is. Get an education. That's what I'm going to do. And we're going to have a real home of our own, right in this county. A 'forever home!' " She looked dreamily into the sky. "A friend of mine, Spud—I told you about him—he gave me a dictionary, so I'm studying even when I'm not going to school."

"Ain't likely to be no school no more fer me nor my family," Twyla said sadly. "We ain't got no clothes fit to wear even if'n Pop got work and kep' us fed and stuff."

"You've got time," Hildy encouraged. "School doesn't start for more than two months yet."

"Time done 'bout run out fer us Hocketts, I think." Twyla turned away from Hildy and walked toward her tent.

Hildy felt sorry for Twyla but didn't know how to help. As she approached the blue tent, Hildy's father drove up with Molly, Mrs. Hockett, and all the kids.

Molly's lips were set in a tight, hard line, and Hildy knew at once that something was wrong. When she jumped up on the running board on the driver's side, she smelled her father's breath. Frightened, she glanced at his eyes and knew the truth. He had not only been drinking, he was drunk.

"No job," he said thickly to Hildy. "No money. No house.

No nothing except this blasted Depression!"

Hildy didn't know what to say. She glanced at her step-mother, who was getting out of the front seat with the baby. Molly kept her eyes down, obviously embarrassed in front of Mrs. Hockett and the kids.

Joe Corrigan staggered slightly as he walked over to the other tent to borrow a fishing line and some tackle from Mr. Hockett. Hildy worried about her father being on the river in his condi-tion. She called to him but he didn't seem to hear.

Hildy helped put the younger kids down for a nap, then she and her stepmother sat outside the tent flap facing the river. The sun had settled below the tallest cottonwood trees, so there was some shade.

Molly darned socks for the girls, her eyes on the work but her voice reaching out. "Hildy, if your father doesn't find work soon, I'm not sure what's going to happen to him or us."

Hildy started sorting socks by sizes and tossing them into piles at her feet. "He'll be all right," she said, trying to sound confident.

"Oh, I'm sure he'll keep us eating—catching fish like he's trying to do now. But what about clothes for school? All you girls got to have decent clothes. I won't have my family looking like ragamuffins. But I can't work because of the baby."

"I'll get a job and help out," Hildy offered.

Molly looked up, startled. "You? No offense, Hildy, but there are no jobs for able-bodied men. What makes you think some-body would hire a twelve-year-old girl?"

"Ruby got a job at Grizzly Gulch."

"Yes, but only for room and board. No money. And that's only for a short time while she looks for her father."

Hildy thought back for a moment to that morning, and slowly the good feeling of the hymn singing returned. Suddenly she remembered her grandparents' encouragement to depend on the Lord. Right now, that was hard to do, but it was all she had.

"The Lord will help us," she said, "as long as I do my part, Molly. Tomorrow I'll see if I can find a job."

Shortly after dawn the next day, Hildy awoke, remembering that it had been just over two weeks since they had left Illinois. Nothing had gone as expected, but she wasn't going to be discouraged. She tried not to think about Don Gridley's threats.

Joe Corrigan had already left in the Lexington Minuteman when Hildy crawled out of the tent where the other girls were still asleep.

Molly poured coffee into a chipped cup with a missing handle. "Your father was ashamed of what he did yesterday," she told Hildy without looking up. "He's a good man, but he's carrying a mighty heavy load. Don't be too harsh in what you think of him." She set the coffeepot back over the fire.

"I won't," Hildy responded sincerely. Walking over to a white pan sitting on an upturned box, she splashed cold water on her face. Sputtering, she said, "I was thinking last night after I said my prayers. I'm going to write my granny back in the Ozarks, and I'm going to write your brother in Oklahoma, too. I mean, I will if you have a couple of three-cent stamps?"

"I think maybe I have. What're you going to write about?"

"I did Granny wrong once, and I need to make that right. And Uncle Cecil—well, he was so good to me when Ruby and I were at the ranch where he works that I just want to thank him."

Molly drank deeply from her coffee cup. "I'm sure they'll both be pleased to hear from you."

"I wish I knew how to contact Spud," Hildy said wistfully. "He's my friend—the boy we met who ran away from his father in New York."

Molly nodded.

"I'd sure like to see Spud again. Maybe I can talk him into writing his family. They must be worried sick about him, not knowing where he's been for a couple years or more."

Molly refilled her cup and smiled. "Hildy, you're making me mighty proud of you."

Hildy didn't know what to say, so she changed the subject. "I think I'll go write those letters now before the kids wake up."

"You'll find stamps and a writing tablet just inside the flap in that box on the right-hand side."

"Thanks," Hildy said, hurrying to find them.

It was midmorning before the kids were fed, dressed, and left in Molly's care. Then Hildy braided her hair, took her letters, and joined Twyla for the three-mile walk into town.

Twyla was unusually quiet as they walked along the paved county road.

"You all right?" Hildy asked in concern.

Twyla broke into sobs and leaned against her friend's shoulder. "Oh, Hildy!" she cried. "I overheard my folks a-talkin' last night when they thought everyone was asleep. They're talkin' 'bout havin' to . . . to give us kids away!"

"They're what?"

"To strangers or anybody'll who'll care for us, 'cause they cain't. And they don't want us to starve."

"Are you kidding me, Twyla?"

"Honest! That's what they said. They've tried all the agencies that's s'posed to help people like us. But those folks say we ain't lived here long enough to be he'ped by the county. The state says we ain't residents, and the fed'ral gov'ment won't he'p, neither."

Hildy shook her head. "Nobody gives their kids away," she protested; "not even in hard times like these! You must've misunderstood."

"No, I didn't." Twyla sniffed. "'Sides, I heerd 'bout it oncet, 'coupla years ago. Really did. Only I never fig'ered it'd happen to us."

"Well, something'll work out, Twyla. Now, stop crying or you'll look a mess when we go inside."

When the girls entered the post office with its barred windows and long rows of boxes, Hildy heard the peeping of baby chicks. "Listen!" she said. "How can they grow chickens in a post office?"

Twyla managed a weak smile. "They don't belong to the post office, silly. Them chicks was shipped through the mail fer some customer to pick up."

"Are you serious?"

"My bonded word. Chicks come in flat boxes 'bout three er four feet square. There's holes cut so's they kin breathe. I've seen 'em here lotsa times."

Hildy walked up to the barred window and stretched to see if the chicks were in sight. They weren't.

The large, balding postal clerk with silver wire-rimmed glasses looked up from sorting mail into patron boxes. "Be right with you, girls."

"No hurry," Hildy replied. She turned to Twyla. "When we get our 'forever home,' if it's not in town, we'll have a farm and raise chickens and have a garden. We'll have a pet, too."

"We never had no pet. Cain't afford to feed one."

"Same with us," Hildy assured her friend. "But we're going to have a dog or cat or something someday. If it's a dog, he'll help protect the garden and chickens. A chicken farm!" she exclaimed with sudden surprise at the idea. "We'll sell the eggs. I saw a sign on that grocery store we passed: 'We Buy Eggs'!"

The postal clerk walked to the other side of the grillwork and looked over the top of his glasses at Hildy. "You must be new to California," he remarked.

"Why, yes. How'd you know?" Hildy asked.

"Out here, they're called ranches, not farms," the clerk replied kindly.

"Really? What's the difference?"

"Name, mostly. Now, what can I do for you girls?"

"I'd like to mail these letters. Already stamped."

The postmaster reached out a thick hand and took the letters. He glanced at the envelopes. "You forgot your name and return address," he said.

"I can put my name, but we don't have an address yet."

"Write *General Delivery* under your name. This town's so small we'll find you if any mail comes for you." He shoved a pen toward her.

Hildy wrote hastily in the upper-left-hand corner and handed the letters back.

The clerk looked at the name. "Corrigan?" he said. "Seems

to me we got some mail for you." Turning sideways, he reached into a cubbyhole.

"For us?" Hildy asked in surprise.

"Yep. Here 'tis." The postmaster read off the address: " 'Miss Hildy Corrigan, General Delivery, Lone River, California.' " He started to hand it over, then asked with a teasing smile, "Who's Spud?"

In glad surprise Hildy grabbed the letter and ran outside with it. Twyla caught up with her friend just as Hildy opened the letter and hastily skimmed it. She let out a happy yell.

"Spud's coming!" she exclaimed. "Says he'll probably be here about the time this letter arrives, so watch for him here at the post office. Come on. I've got to tell Molly."

Hildy and Twyla ran most of the way back to the campsite by the bridge. Hildy was so excited that she babbled away about Spud, telling Twyla everything she could remember about him. Twyla got caught up in Hildy's enthusiasm, so neither girl mentioned the terrible possibility that Twyla's parents would have to give away their children in order for them to survive.

The girls scrambled down a steep, dusty trail from the corner of the rusty trestle bridge. As they reached level ground and ran across the sand and stones toward the tents, all the younger children from both tents came running and yelling to meet them.

Elizabeth outran the others, panting as she collapsed against Hildy's knees. "Guess what, Hildy?"

"What?"

"Daddy's got a job!"

"A job?" Hildy almost dropped Spud's letter.

All the other sisters joined in a happy chorus, confirming the news.

Elizabeth's eyes sparkled. "He's also found a place for us to live."

"A house?" Hildy grabbed Elizabeth and Martha's hands and swung them around in a wild, happy dance. "A home! A home!"

Elizabeth stopped suddenly, shaking her head. "It's not a home," she said softly. "It's a barn!"

CHAPTER ELEVEN

THREATS FROM A HORSEMAN

Hildy blinked in surprise and bent to look directly into her sister's serious eyes. "A barn?"

"Ask Daddy yourself," Elizabeth challenged, starting to turn away. Then she spun back around. "You promised us a 'forever home,' " she said accusingly, "not a barn!"

Hildy drew back as though slapped in the face. "Listen!" she exclaimed. "I want a real home as much as anybody. And we'll get one, too. We've just got to have faith and keep working toward that goal."

Hildy's other sisters weren't satisfied.

Martha scuffed her bare foot in the dust. "A barn's for animals, not people," she mumbled.

For a second, Hildy didn't know what to say. She glanced imploringly at Twyla.

Twyla gathered the younger girls close to her. "A barn ain't so bad," she said wistfully. "Some people 'round here's livin' in chicken houses. Fact is, I wisht we had either a chicken house or a barn 'steada this here ol' tent." She motioned toward her family's shelter by the bridge.

Hildy managed a smile. "Sure. A barn's better than *our* tent, too. Come on. Let's go talk to Daddy." Grabbing Iola's and Sarah's hands, she started skipping over the sand. "Don't make Daddy feel bad by complaining," she cautioned. "Be real proud of him for getting a job."

Twyla went on to her tent while Hildy ran with her four younger sisters to the campsite. Joe Corrigan stood in front of the tent flap talking to Molly.

Relief flooded Hildy's heart to see her father's eyes bright and his face smiling. She ran to him and threw her arms around him. "What kind of job is it, Daddy?"

"Oh, I'll be doing a little buckerooing for the Wood Brothers Ranches."

"What's buckerooing?"

"Cowboying," her father said with a laugh. "Like Molly's brother, your Uncle Cecil, does in Oklahoma. I'll be rounding up cattle, and riding fences'n all in the foothills about ten miles east of here."

"On a horse?" little Iola asked, wide-eyed.

"On a big horse!" her father assured her. "And the boss says he's got a barn-house near town. We can live there 'til we find a real house."

"A barn-house?" Hildy asked.

"That's what Mr. Wood called it. He and his family used to live in the main house that burned down. So while they were building the place where they now live, they fixed up the barn enough to stay in. Since then, hired hands have slept there sometimes since the ranch doesn't have a bunkhouse. So if it's good enough for all those folks, it'll be good enough for us 'til we can do better."

"When can we move in?" Hildy asked, fingering Spud's letter excitedly. She was anxious to tell them about his coming, but the news about her dad's job and a place to live were more important right now.

"Be a while yet," he said, squatting down on his heels. It was a sitting position Hildy had often seen men take when they worked outdoors a lot and there were no rocks or stumps on which to sit. "It's got to be fixed up some."

"What's it like?" Hildy asked, dropping to the sand in front of her father and arranging her long dress across her legs.

"Oh, it's got a wood floor and glass windows where they used to be open, like most barns. The main thing's that we'll have a better shelter than this tent. There are about three acres where the kids can play—all fenced and planted with ladino clover. That's a fast-growing clover farmers use for hay or grazing cattle. Maybe we can have a milk cow and plant a garden."

Iola grinned up at her daddy shyly. "Could we have a pet?"

Her father scooped her up in his arms and balanced her on his knee. "I suppose we could, but it'd have to be one that scrounged food for itself. We can barely afford to feed ourselves, let alone a dog or something."

"A cat!" exclaimed the ever-practical Elizabeth. "It could catch mice and gophers."

"Mice?" Martha shuddered. "Does the barn have mice?"

"Probably," her father said matter-of-factly. "It seems that mice are everywhere these days. But I'll take them over rats."

"Rats?" Martha fairly shrieked. "Will we have them, too?"

"I hope not," her father answered. "But whatever the situation is, we'll make do until we can afford a real house."

Molly fed some sticks into the open fire where she was starting to prepare the noon meal. "Tell them about the chicken pen, Joe."

"Oh, yes. I almost forgot. Kids, we can also raise a few chickens for eggs and eating."

"Baby chicks?" Hildy cried. "Oh, Daddy, can we raise our own? There were some at the post office today. And I found out we can order them by mail." Quickly she told them everything she had learned about the little chicks at the post office.

When she finished, her father gently pushed Iola from his knee and stood up. "We'll talk about that after I've taken all of you over to see the place."

"When? When?" the girls cried together.

"Don't know yet. Now let's eat so I can get back. I start work this afternoon."

The kids were each given a cold boiled potato to eat. Molly had boiled the potatoes the day before over the open fire. She had also tried to cook some beans but had been unable to keep the fire going at a high enough temperature for hours. As a result, the beans weren't done. But Molly heated the liquid and poured it off as soup to go with the potatoes.

When the meal was over and Joe Corrigan had driven across the shallow river crossing to go to work, Hildy told her stepmother about Spud's letter.

"He's been working with your brother in Oklahoma," Hildy explained. "Spud even calls him Uncle Cecil now, and he said that as soon as he gets his first paycheck, he's heading for California."

Molly smiled as Hildy rushed on.

"He said he'd go to the post office and ask where we live, so we need to watch for him there. But it'll be hard to get into town if Daddy's working out toward the foothills."

"We'll find a way to watch for him," Molly promised.

Iola leaned her head back to look up into Hildy's face. "Is Spud your boyfriend?" she asked in tiny voice.

Molly laughed. "Your sister's not old enough to have a boyfriend, Iola. Spud's just a nice young man she met in the Ozarks, and he's coming out to California on a visit."

As Hildy washed the dishes from the noon meal, she thought about what Molly had said concerning Spud. Maybe she was too young to have a boyfriend, but she *was* really looking forward to seeing him again.

It was Martha's turn to dry the dishes. And since she didn't particularly want to be drying dishes when she could be playing, she worked halfheartedly in silence, giving Hildy a lot of time to think. Molly had put Sarah and Iola down for a nap in the tent while Elizabeth went to visit the girls at the Hockett tent.

Washing each dish carefully, Hildy set it on an upturned

wooden lug box that once had held peaches. Suddenly a flash of sunlight reflected off something, hitting Hildy in the eyes. Shading her eyes, she looked up to see where the light was coming from.

"It's Don Gridley," she told her little sister. "He's watching us again."

"Wish Ruby was here," Martha said. "She'd run him off."

"I think he's spying on us because he's watching for her. He wants to get even with Ruby because she pulled him around by his hair."

"I remember," Martha bent over with laughter. "Wish she'd come do it agin!"

"I wish it hadn't happened," Hildy said seriously. "That made Don mad. And I didn't help by running his horse off, along with the other horses belonging to Don's three friends."

Martha stopped laughing. "How'd you do that?"

Hildy briefly recounted what had happened at the brush arbor. When she finished, she saw that Don was still sitting on his horse across the fence, watching the camp.

Martha looked up at him, too. "He makes me nervous, spying like that," she muttered.

"Me, too." Hildy handed the last dish to her sister and wiped her hands on her apron. "I think I'll go talk to him."

"He might hurt you!"

"I don't think so. He's on the other side of the fence, so it should be all right."

"Just the same, I'm going to follow you to make sure."

"Okay, but stay back unless he crosses the fence. Then you run tell Molly."

Hildy made her way along the riverbank, past the shallow ford, beyond the deep hole where Mr. Hockett had his trotline, and on to the barbed-wire fence that ended at the water.

Don Gridley sat casually on his horse, watching Hildy's approach. "Try to stay downwind from me!" he called.

Hildy bristled at the suggestion that she smelled bad. She had always taken a "sponge bath" every day, washing herself from face to feet out of a small pan. Her late mother used to say, "We're not rich, but we are clean." Molly felt the same way, so the Corrigan kids were never dirty.

"Why're you hanging around, watching us?" Hildy asked, struggling to keep her voice calm.

"I told you. I don't like Okies, Arkies, hillbillies, and the rest of you people from out of state."

Hildy remembered a word she'd learned that morning from Spud's dictionary. "You're a bigot," she said evenly.

He stirred in the saddle and frowned down at her. "What does that mean?"

"Someone who is very intolerant of anything that isn't his own."

"You mean, like you?"

"I'm from the Ozarks, yes. But I'm just as good a person as you or anybody else!" Hildy's words were more emphatic than she had intended. She softened her tone. "But a bigot can also be against a belief or race, like you were about the people in that brush arbor."

"I don't care about any church!" he snapped. "And I sure don't like the flood of poor white trash like you that's been pouring over this county lately."

"Didn't your folks come here from somewhere else?" Hildy challenged.

"They came here with the Gold Rush," the boy said with pride. He leaned across the saddle pommel and sneered. "Anyway, I hate what all you fruit tramps are doing to this land."

"When your ancestors arrived with the Gold Rush, they came from somewhere else," Hildy said in a reasonable tone. "They stayed and built up the land. My family's trying to do the same thing."

"It's not the same!" Don exploded. "Look at you. Barefooted. Old patched dress. Still wearing braids at your age."

Hildy hadn't meant to get into an argument with the boy. She shrugged. "I imagine your '49 ancestors were dirt poor when they arrived, too."

"My father says you Okies don't have the will to do anything. So you're not like us at all." He leaned forward to look down on her with angry eyes. "I'd like to run all of you out of here for good!"

Hildy stirred uneasily as the boy leaned over the saddle horn and showed his teeth in an angry grimace. "What did they ever do to you?" she asked. "In fact, what did *I* ever do to you?"

"You know what you did. You spooked our horses. And that hillbilly friend of yours pulled me around by my hair. If she wasn't a girl, I'd have busted her good."

Hildy started to remind Don that he had swung his fists at Ruby, and Ruby had kept him at arms' length with her powerful grip.

But Don added through clenched teeth, "I've got a good mind to come over that fence and throw you in the river."

Hildy forced herself to show no fear. She tried speaking quietly. "My father's found us a place to live. We're moving away, so you probably won't ever see us again."

"Good." Don relaxed a little and leaned back in the saddle, his left hand resting on the horse's rump. "To the Ozarks, I hope?"

"No, to a place owned by the Woods Brothers."

"Ah, that house burned down some time back."

"The barn didn't."

For a moment, the boy frowned, then shook his head. "I should have known. Hillbillies living in a barn."

"It's a barn-house! Besides, it's better than our tent."

"You're right," he nodded, pausing slightly. "Say, maybe the boys—the ones whose horses you ran off with mine—and I should give you a welcome."

Hildy swallowed hard, instantly sorry that she had told Don about the barn-house. She didn't know what he might do, but it worried her.

Suddenly, there was a shriek behind Hildy and a splash. She spun around, seeing a white spray in the deep part of the river. For a second she thought it might be a big fish.

Then she remembered her sister. Hildy's eyes frantically searched the shore. There was no sign of Martha!

Hildy's gaze snapped back to the river. The water had settled except for a few big bubbles, some small branches, and a few broken twigs. All were swept rapidly downstream.

"Martha!" Hildy screamed, running along the riverbank toward the bubbles.

CHAPTER TWELVE

DANGER IN THE RIVER

Hildy raced along the riverbank, her frightened eyes focused on the bubbles and debris floating on the surface of the swift, dark waters.

With a desperate prayer, Hildy tore her eyes from the river and shot frantic glances along the bank again in hopes of seeing her little sister. Instead, both families came pouring out of the tents near the bridge, attracted by Hildy's terrified scream.

There was no doubt. Martha had fallen into the river. The only clue to her whereabouts was the surface bubbles, now almost gone, and the twigs and dry branches bobbing rapidly downstream.

Hildy could not swim. She had dog paddled a little in various small creeks, yet she was certainly not a swimmer. But Hildy didn't think of that. She knew only that her little sister was drowning, and nobody else except Don was close enough to save her.

Hildy plunged wildly through an opening of the wispy, thin willows toward a downed cottonwood tree. It lay partway into the river, directly in the path of the surface debris and bubbles.

Hildy sprang up on the end of the log resting on shore.

Ignoring the rough bark cutting into her bare feet, she stumbled along the log out over the river. The log rolled slightly under Hildy's weight. She threw her arms out to balance herself and threaded her way through the dry branches and leaves to the far end of the log.

It dipped dangerously under her weight as she neared what had been the treetop. The branches snagged her clothes and tore her flesh, but she didn't seem to notice.

When she could go no farther, she stopped. Breathing hard from fear and exertion, her eyes darted frantically upstream. "Oh, Lord, no!" Her heart sank. There was no sign of her sister.

The bubbles were now gone. The current had separated the broken limbs and twigs, and they bobbed safely along the far shore, free from the turbulent river.

Hildy screamed, and started to sob. "Martha! Oh, Martha!" Blinking back tears, Hildy looked anxiously for some sign of her sister but saw only the river, dark and swift, sliding by with little gurgling sounds. Nothing was left behind except traces of foam near the far shore.

Hildy's legs suddenly seemed like wet spaghetti. They started to collapse under her dress.

Then a flash of color upstream caught Hildy's eye. She raised her head quickly, wiped her tears away with her hands and stared.

That's her dress! Dashing back off the log, she ignored her cut and bleeding hands and feet. She jumped onto the riverbank and ran a few feet upstream to where she had glimpsed a piece of Martha's dress. It was no bigger than a hand, something that almost popped to the surface, then was sucked back under the menacing water. But it offered hope.

Hildy saw people running toward her as she tried to push her way through the underbrush. Forcing her slender body through some young willows to reach the river's edge, she stood, panting and terribly afraid, on the bank, desperately searching the area where she had glimpsed the piece of dress.

There was nothing. The river was dark and deep, keeping its secret from Hildy's frantic, probing eyes.

Faintly, she heard Twyla's voice. "I'm coming, Hildy! I'm coming!"

Hildy moaned in despair, her darting glances seeing nothing of her sister.

Then, slowly, like a teasing, mocking motion from the river, another hand-sized piece of Martha's dress floated into sight. It did not break the surface but instantly sank again.

That was enough for Hildy. She sprang feet first into the shockingly cold water. Hildy sucked in her breath sharply, then sank like a stone, surprised how deep the river was so close to the bank.

Still holding her breath against the numbing cold, Hildy grabbed desperately for the piece of her sister's dress. Nothing.

She opened her eyes under water, but it was so dark she had only a vague sense of light above her head. Still, she groped frantically, hoping . . . hoping.

Suddenly, her left hand touched something—a piece of cloth. Hildy closed her fingers and held on. The cloth didn't come easily, so Hildy knew she had caught some part of her sister's clothing. Hildy swiveled her body and brought her right hand around to grip the garment alongside her other hand.

Then, dying for a breath of air, Hildy kicked wildly with her feet. Her head broke the surface. She gulped loudly, taking in the sweetest breath of her life. Then she tugged hard on Martha's dress, trying to pull her sister to the surface.

Sobbing with fear, Hildy tried to suck in more air but choked on the water pouring into her mouth. Fighting a coughing spasm, she pulled fast, hand over hand, on the garment still out of sight under the water.

Finally she brought up the torn hem of Martha's dress. Automatically, Hildy reached down to where she thought her sister's waist would be. Feeling around quickly, her face under water, Hildy found a limp arm. She grabbed it and pulled, jerking her own head above the surface.

Martha's face came up a second later, head rolling loosely against her chest. Her light blond hair swayed a moment in the current, then draped itself wetly across her face.

Oh, my Lord! Hildy thought. *She's dead!*

Still, Hildy hung on to her sister's lifeless form. Gagging and coughing from the water, Hildy desperately tried to breathe. She struggled weakly toward the shore a couple feet away.

Suddenly, a hand reached out from the riverbank and closed on Hildy's long left braid. A sharp pull seemed to almost yank her head off.

She heard Twyla's triumphant voice. "Gotcha!"

Moments later, many hands reached out to help. Mr. Hockett grabbed Hildy's arm and jerked her halfway onto the shore. A second later, he yanked Martha up beside Hildy.

Hildy was still choking and sobbing for breath. As she struggled to her hands and knees, her eyes stung, and she couldn't see well. Yet she caught a glimpse of a horse and rider beyond the fence.

Through this whole ordeal Don Gridley hadn't moved.

Mr. Hockett grabbed Martha's limp form in his arms, then stood up and ran back to the downed cottonwood log. Hildy tried to follow, but she was too weak. She vaguely heard excited voices, including those of Molly and all the kids from both the Hockett and Corrigan tents.

Hildy's unbelieving eyes snapped back to Don Gridley. He turned his horse from the fence and rode slowly away. He had been close to the tragedy, but he had not moved to help.

Hildy spun back to her sister as Mr. Hockett laid Martha face down across the butt end of the log on the shore.

Above the excited voices, Twyla shouted to Hildy. "He's rollin' her to git the water outta her lungs!" she cried.

Hildy had heard of that being done to drowning victims, but she didn't know if it worked. She struggled to her feet and staggered toward the log.

All of a sudden Martha made a coughing sound, then let out a strangled cry.

Mr. Hockett looked up. "She's alive!" he shouted. "She's goin' to be all right!"

Hildy collapsed beside her sister, hugging her with relief.

Later that day, Martha rested from her near-drowning experience while the other kids were playing. Hildy and Twyla sat alone on the bank of the shallow river ford. For several minutes, they stared silently, thoughtfully into the water.

Twyla finally spoke. "No use a-thinkin' no more 'bout it, Hildy. Martha's fine and soon y'all be a-movin' away from this ol' river."

Hildy nodded but continued to stare. The water was so clear and shallow here that she could see the bottom well out into the stream. But when the girl lifted her eyes downstream, the water was deep, black, and threatening—still waiting . . . waiting . . .

Hildy shivered and looked away. She turned to her friend. "When do you think you're going to move from here?"

Twyla shrugged and smoothed her patched old dress over her knees. Like Hildy's, Twyla's knees had fresh cuts from the rescue efforts. "Don't rightly know," she said. "Pop still ain't got no job."

Hildy wanted to ask if there had been any more talk about the parents giving away the Hockett children, but she changed her mind. She leaned back on her hands. "You suppose Spud's got to town yet?" she asked.

"Not 'less'n he hitchhiked from Oklahoma faster'n the U.S. mail." Twyla grinned and playfully touched Hildy's scratched arm. "Ye like him a lot, huh?"

Hildy thought a moment before answering. "He's nice."

"How ye reckon him'n Don Gridley'll git along?"

"I'm not going to tell Spud about Don."

Twyla's voice held genuine surprise. "No?"

"No."

"Not even 'bout today when Don sat right there on his horse and watched you and Martha purt' near get drownded?"

Hildy stirred uneasily. "There's something seriously wrong with that boy. You ever hear of anybody who wouldn't try to help a couple of drowning people?"

"Reckon not."

"Twyla, that kid really scares me!"

Twyla started to answer when a shout from the camps caused the girls to look up. Hildy's father was easing along the narrow dirt lane toward the far bank.

Hildy got up stiffly, pained by the soreness in her body. "Guess he's coming home early to take us to see the barn-house. I can hardly wait!"

"Wisht I could go with ye to see it." Twyla got to her feet, making a face at the pain from a cut in her hand. "Bet it's a whole lot nicer'n these ol' tents."

"I wish you could go, too," Hildy said. "Maybe Daddy'll take you after he hears how you helped save Martha. Come on, let's go find out."

Everyone talked at once, telling Joe Corrigan about the near-drowning incident. Hildy chose not to mention the calloused, uncaring way Don Gridley had watched and then ridden away. Hildy wasn't sure what her father would do, but she didn't want him tangling with the Gridleys and maybe getting on their blacklist, as Twyla's father was.

Joe Corrigan hugged and kissed Hildy and Martha until they were embarrassed. Hildy pulled free of her father's arms. "Can we take Twyla with us to see the barn-house?" she asked.

"Guess so, Hildy. Ruby's not here, so Twyla can have her place in the car."

Later, when the crowded Lexington Minuteman turned off the paved road onto a poplar-lined dirt road, Hildy had mixed feelings. *I never dreamed I'd look forward to seeing a barn for a home*, she thought. *But I guess anything's better than living by that river*.

From the front seat, Joe Corrigan announced, "Soon as we pass the last tree, you'll see the barn off to the right."

Hildy turned with Twyla and all the Corrigan family to catch a glimpse of the strange home.

Martha pointed. "There!" she shouted, seeming back to normal. "Oh, it's a *big* ol' barn."

"Just a regular barn," her father answered. "Except for the eastern part that's been fixed up some. See the glass window that's been cut in the sliding door? Over to the left."

Iola took one look and stomped her foot. "I hate it," she said emphatically, turning accusing eyes on Hildy. "You promised us a 'forever home'!"

Hildy tried not to be hurt by the remark. She studied the weathered old barn. It hadn't been painted in years, and on the north side of the roof, there was moss growing on the eaves. The roof line sagged in the center like a sway-back mule.

As Hildy's own disappointment grew, she caught a whiff of a terrible, sickening odor.

"Daddy," she cried, "what's that?"

The other kids turned away in disgust. "Phew!" they yelled. "What stinks?"

Their father made a face. "Rotten eggs!" He lifted his hand from the steering wheel and pointed. "See those streaks down the walls? Somebody's thrown a bunch of rotten eggs. That happened since I was here earlier today."

"Oh, Joe!" Molly exclaimed. "Who would do a terrible thing like that?"

Hildy and Twyla exchanged glances, and their mouths moved together in forming the name *Don Gridley*!

—

CHAPTER THIRTEEN

THE BARN-HOUSE

Hildy walked with her family and Twyla upwind of the splintered, sagging old barn. The stench of rotten eggs broken against the gray boards wasn't as bad with the wind blowing from behind them toward the barn. It would have been unbearable inside, so they had to be satisfied to view the outside of the barn from a distance.

Hildy was disappointed about not being able to see inside the barn-house, but she tried to hide her feelings. Although she didn't want anybody to know, she was actually more concerned about Don Gridley than the barn-house. "There's a garden hose next to the sliding door," she said, trying to be cheerful. "We can wash most of the eggs off, can't we, Daddy?"

"Should help," he agreed. "I'll do that while the rest of you look around."

Molly said she would stay with her husband and stand in the shade of a big Chinaberry tree to protect baby Joey from the sun. Hildy's sisters ran ahead, shouting about who should be first to look in the other side of the barn and the various out-buildings—the corral, sheds, outhouse, and tank house.

Hildy and Twyla walked behind, thoughtfully looking over the ranch while keeping a watchful eye on the kids.

Hildy pointed to the left about a hundred yards. "That's where the house stood before it burned, I guess. The stone chimney's still standing," she said. "Those look like wild blackberry bushes over there, too. They've about covered the foundation, it looks like."

Twyla shaded her eyes against the afternoon sun. "Pump house looks in purty good shape. Win'mill's got a coupla vanes missin', but the wheel's still turnin'. Works, too. I kin hear the water fallin' down in the tank."

Hildy walked into the shade of the two-story-tall tank house that stood next to the windmill. On the lower floor, the tank house door sagged open. The interior was dark and gloomy except for a single shaft of sunshine, which glistened in the distinctive webs of poisonous black widow spiders. A musty smell drifted to Hildy's nose.

She looked up. The tank house was weathered. It needed paint, and some boards were missing above, where the storage tank was.

Hildy watched as the hot afternoon breeze hit the aluminum sails of the windmill on top. They were staggered in a circular pattern so that they caught the slightest wind. With each turn of the sails, the unoiled gears squealed in protest.

Hildy took a couple steps toward the windmill's metal supports. Then ducking under them, she touched the pipe that came out of the ground and ran up to the tank house. "It's cold," she announced. "We'll have plenty of water for everything, including a garden, our chickens, and the pet we're going to get."

"Have ye decided on what kinda pet?" Twyla asked, inspecting stacks of old newspapers in a corner.

Hildy shrugged. "Don't know yet." She raised her eyes to the fenced green pasture, dotted with low-growing white blossoms. "Wonder if there's enough grass to support a horse."

Twyla laughed. "That's not grass. That's ladino clover. It's watered by the snow that melts in the spring an' comes down those ditches over there. See? Anyway, a horse ain't a pet. You need a dog, especially if Don Gridley comes sneakin' 'round agin."

Hildy's thoughts jumped back to that morning and the way the Gridley boy had behaved when she and her sister were almost drowning. "Wonder why he hates people like us so much."

"Some folks seem to like hatin' other folks," Twyla mused. She stopped to peer under a clump of blackberry vines leading away from the tank house. The vines were as high as a housetop and stretched away like a giant green worm for about a hundred yards. "Bet they's cottontails in here," she said.

Hildy came close and bent over to look. "You mean rabbits?"

"Small eatin' kind. Not those long-eared jackrabbits ye see everywhere in open country. Cottontails like brush and ledges an' such-like places."

"I couldn't hurt a little rabbit," Hildy replied firmly.

"If'n this Depression continues long enough, ye may be plumb glad to eat rabbit or whatever ye git yore hands on. Oh, look! Yonder's a box trap."

Hildy drew closer and bent to see where Twyla was pointing. The trap was a simple box-like unit about two feet long. It had wooden sides, top and bottom, with stout wire mesh on the back end. Hildy could see that the trap was empty, although the wooden trapdoor was closed. "How does it work?" she asked.

"Ye raise this here wooden end in the slots or grooves, like this." She demonstrated. "That makes the door stand up above the trap so's the end is open. The rabbit goes in to nibble on some carrots or whatever bait ye have. Then when he does that, the trigger's released, and the door slides down into place. See? The rabbit cain't git out. Cain't git hurt, neither."

Hildy smiled in wonder.

The girls turned back then, herding the younger sisters ahead of them. As they approached the barn, Hildy's father was coiling up the old, cracked hose around a faucet sticking up at the corner of the building.

"Sorry, kids," he announced. "I've washed all the eggs off I can get, but it still smells too bad to go inside. We'll have to come back in a few days and hope the stink is gone by then."

The sun had already set by the time the Lexington Minuteman eased into the shallow river and crawled out on the other side. Hildy saw Mr. Hockett wading in the river, taking catfish off his trotline. Twyla's mother and brothers and sisters came running out of the tent to ask about the barn-house.

After the rotten egg incident had been discussed at length in the deep shadows of the cottonwoods, Twyla's father spoke up. "Joe, y'all air mighty lucky to have a job an' a place to live, like that thar barn. Now y'all have a-plenty fer school clothes an' such things, too."

Hildy's father shook his head. "I'm making just enough at buckerooing to feed my family and buy a little gas for the car. With what little that pays, I'll need a second job to buy school clothes for the kids."

Mrs. Hockett smiled sadly. "Don't hardly seem right to hold down two jobs whilst my man cain't find even one. 'Course, he tries, but his bum back goes out on him real easy, ye see. Nobody wants to hire 'im."

Hildy saw her father's mouth open quickly as though he were going to say something, but he closed it so sharply his teeth snapped. Hildy had the distinct impression that her father had almost said something he might have been thinking for some time.

Hildy had thought it, too. Why didn't Mr. Hockett ever go out looking for work? All he did was fish or complain because he wasn't working.

But Hildy liked Twyla too much to say anything that might hurt her feelings. Besides, Twyla seemed as certain as her father that the reason Mr. Hockett couldn't work was because the Gridleys had warned everyone in town not to hire him. Hildy didn't believe that. But when a person's mind was made up, Hildy knew that talking sense didn't change anything.

Twyla looked at her father. "I saw a sign fer 'cot pickers when we was a-drivin' back from seein' the barn-house," she said.

"Cot?" Hildy asked.

"Apricots," Mrs. Hockett replied. "Hard work, but pays good if'n ye kin move a twelve-foot ladder 'round an orchard and if'n ye pick fast. Best thing is to work in the cuttin' sheds."

Hildy looked puzzled and Twyla explained. "Oh, that there's a place where they dry the 'cots after they're picked. Ye cut the 'cots with a knife and remove the pit. Then ye put the two halves on a tray. That's taken to a little shed where they burn sulphur to keep the bugs off. Finally, the trays of 'cots are put out in the sun to dry."

Hildy's hopes rose. "Could I get a job cutting 'cots?"

Mrs. Hockett shook her head. "S'posed to be fourteen years old."

"Oh," said Hildy.

Molly looked at the baby asleep in her arms. "If I didn't have to stay with Joey, maybe I could get a job in the cutting sheds," she said wistfully.

Twyla's eyes brightened. "I knowed a girl oncet who put on boys' clothes and got a job pickin' peaches," she told them. "Fooled ol' man Gridley all summer!"

Hildy grimaced. "The Gridleys own orchards and sheds as well as cattle ranches?"

Mrs. Hockett snorted. "Reckon they do. 'Spect they own 'bout ever'thin', 'ceptin' the Wood Brothers Ranches. That's why the Gridleys and the Woods don't git along any better'n two polecats in a gunny sack."

Hildy fingered the end of one of her long, brown braids. "When my cousin Ruby and I were coming to California, we dressed up in boys' overalls so nobody knew we were girls."

Twyla laughed. "How'd ye hide yore hair?"

"Under a hat. Worked fine, too."

Twyla eyed her suspiciously. "I don't know 'bout that."

Hildy soon discovered that her father was serious about trying to find more work. The next day he left early to apply for a second job before going to work on the Wood Brothers cattle ranch. He didn't return until dusk that night.

Hildy and Twyla were sitting on a high boulder, talking, when Hildy saw her father's headlights bouncing off the shallow part of the river. She and Twyla slid off the boulder and ran to meet him. The other Corrigan and Hockett children trailed along behind them, all shouting greetings.

As everyone waited on the bank for the touring sedan to pull out of the water, Twyla grabbed Hildy's hand. "Look! Over by the fence. Don's watchin' us agin."

"Wonder why," Hildy mused. "Do you suppose he feels guilty because he didn't try to help Martha and me?"

"More'n likely he's up to no good," Twyla said darkly. "Oh, yore father's stoppin'. Let's go see if he got that other job."

He hadn't, but he was in a cheerful mood. He carried Iola in one arm while Sarah clung to his free hand. Martha and Elizabeth skipped alongside, and everyone talked at once.

Hildy was glad that since her father had landed a job, he hadn't once come home with the smell of alcohol on his breath.

That night after Molly and Hildy had put all the children to bed, Joe Corrigan carried the lamp outside the blue tent. Placing it on an old stump, he sat down on a log to talk with his wife.

Hildy yawned and went off a few steps into the darkness to say her prayers. She liked to be alone when talking to God.

Hildy prayed with a thankful heart. Her father had a job. Martha had been saved from drowning. The family had a place to stay. Of course, it wasn't what Hildy had expected, but she tried to be grateful for the barn-house anyway. She prayed for Don Gridley, too, fearing his strange behavior.

As Hildy prayed, she felt a hope and excitement she hadn't known in some time. Soon the rotten egg smell would be gone from the barn-house, and the family could move away from the dangerous river. Maybe the Hocketts could also move away.

Then Hildy remembered Spud and asked the Lord to take care of him as he traveled to Lone River.

Hildy was almost ready to say amen at the end of her prayer when she had another thought. Looking up, she added, *Lord, if I could get a job, maybe Daddy wouldn't have to take a night job to*

*buy school clothes for all of us kids. Tomorrow I'm going to try, but I'd
sure like to not have any trouble with Don Gridley or his father. Amen.*

Hildy's hopes rose even higher as she walked back into the
circle of light from the lamp.

Her father looked up and smiled tenderly, taking his gold
watch from the bib pocket of his blue overalls. He held the watch
in his palm and let the fob, a plain leather strap with a metal
end having the word *Caterpillar* on it, hang over the back of his
hand. The leather fob was a replacement for the original gold
chain.

"Bedtime, Hildy," her father said.

Hildy knew that pocket watch and chain had belonged to
her great-grandfather, and it had been passed down until Hildy's father received it when he was about thirteen. Before the
baby had been born, Hildy had thought that she might be next
in line. She had often held the watch and enjoyed listening to
its ticking. But now she supposed that Joey, being a boy, would
probably get it someday.

Molly picked up the lamp and led the way for all of them
back to the tent. Then she placed the lamp just inside the tent
flap on the end of a lug box that had a picture of tomatoes on
it. Molly had told her that the lug, which she had gotten from
a little store in town, had originally been used to haul tomatoes
to the cannery twenty miles away. Now it served as a night
stand.

Hildy watched her father carefully lay his watch down beside
the lamp. It was the one item of value that Joe Corrigan owned.
Hildy knew that her father would have long ago traded the
watch for food if it hadn't been for its sentimental value.

Kissing her father and stepmother goodnight, Hildy crawled
past her sleeping baby brother and her sisters to the pallet at
the back of the tent. Her father blew out the lamp, and soft
darkness filled the crowded tent. Crickets sang in the grass outside, and soon everyone was asleep.

The next morning, Hildy awoke to hear her father whispering fiercely to Molly. "I tell you my watch is gone! It's been
stolen!"

CHAPTER
FOURTEEN

A TERRIBLE SECRET

Hildy sat up quickly on her pallet of boughs and old blankets. "How could your watch be stolen?" she asked.

Her father turned toward her. He was fully dressed in his blue work shirt, faded jeans, wide-brimmed cowboy hat, and scuffed cowboy boots. "I don't know how, but it's gone," he answered angrily. "And it didn't get up and walk off by itself."

Molly stood next to her husband in her long nightgown, her hair still tousled. "Oh, Joe, who'd steal your watch?"

He shrugged. "I hate to think it, but there's nobody around here except our neighbors over there." He pointed toward the other tent.

"The Hocketts?" Molly protested. "No, Joe. They're flat broke, but they're nice people. They wouldn't have stolen your watch."

"Then who?" he demanded.

Molly shook her head. "I don't have any idea."

Hildy started to tell them that Don Gridley might have, but she checked herself. She was afraid of what her father might do, especially since Don hadn't lifted a finger to help save the girls from drowning. "Daddy, I'll help look for your watch," she offered. "Maybe it'll turn up yet."

She searched by herself until her sisters awoke. Then they joined her, but there was no sign of the gold watch. When Twyla came over, she and her brothers and sisters helped search, too. Hildy was sure from the Hocketts' behavior and words that they were as baffled as the Corrigans about where the watch had gone.

When the search was abandoned, Hildy walked with Twyla toward the Hocketts' tent. Twyla's father shuffled slowly toward his old Studebaker, his head down. Mrs. Hockett tried to hide within the deep sunbonnet she always wore outdoors, but Hildy noticed the woman rubbing her eyes. "Something wrong with your folks?" she asked her friend.

"Don't rightly know. They didn't sleep much. I know that. I woke up in the night and heerd 'em a-whisperin'. Mama was a-cryin' real soft-like, but when I sat up and asked if she was sick, they both tol' me to go back to sleep."

Hildy felt uneasy, remembering what Twyla had said Monday morning about her parents possibly giving away the children. Hildy wondered if Twyla had forgotten that, or if she was simply refusing to think about it.

Later, Molly and Mrs. Hockett came back from where they had been hanging freshly washed diapers on the willows to dry.

"Girls," Mrs. Hockett said, "I heard tell yestiddy that they's a doin's over at that brush arbor church all day. Molly and me's a-goin' an' takin' all the kids. Y'all wanna come, too?"

Hildy and Twyla briefly talked it over.

Hildy shook her head. "Since we don't have to watch the kids, Twyla and I'd like to walk into town and see if Spud's showed up yet. Okay?"

After both mothers gave permission, Hildy and Twyla put on their shoes as protection against the hot paved road. Climbing the steep dirt trail up to the edge of the bridge, they walked across it.

Only then did Hildy feel free to tell Twyla she suspected that

Don Gridley had stolen the watch.

"Oh, I cain't believe that," Twyla said. "Don's a no-'ccount, that's fer shore, but why would he steal from po' folks like us?"

"Maybe to get even," Hildy guessed.

Twyla shook her head. "No, I don't rightly think so. He'd be more likely to do somethin' mean to a person, not jist steal one little ol' thing like a watch—even if it's gold."

Soon the baffled girls turned their conversation to Spud, and Hildy felt her heartbeat quicken. "I sure hope he's waiting for us in town," she said, trying not to sound too excited.

As the two friends walked toward town, Hildy kept looking at the big houses on the hilltops overlooking the river. She pointed to a two-story white house with fancy trim. "I wouldn't mind living in a house like that," she said. "Daddy says that's a Victorian style. Maybe I'd live there forever."

"I'd be plumb happy to jist have any home," Twyla replied wistfully.

Hildy reached over and patted her friend's arm. "You'll get a place someday, just as my family will."

Twyla changed the subject. "Say, since we're goin' close to the cuttin' sheds, why don't we try to git us a job?"

"You know we're too young," Hildy objected.

"Won't hurt to try, will it?"

"No, I guess not."

As the girls turned off the county road into a wide, flat area, the smell of burning sulphur from the curing sheds made their eyes water. They approached the low, open-sided shed where women and a few teenage girls and boys were cutting apricots.

When Hildy and Twyla entered a small office in one corner of the shed, a small, dark woman with quick, almost-black eyes looked up. "How old?" she asked without greeting them. Her accent indicated that she was foreign born.

For a moment, they hesitated. Hildy felt tempted to say *fourteen*, but she didn't. "Twelve," she replied.

"Thirteen." Twyla also told the truth.

The woman shook her head with irritation. "Come back

when you're fourteen." She turned to some paperwork spread out before her on the desk.

The two friends slowly walked away from the office, reluctant to leave the cool shade of the cutting sheds for the hot sun. The air was heavy with the smell of ripe and overripe fruit. The overripe apricots attracted swarms of gnats, and both girls had to keep brushing the nuisances from their faces.

"Look how those people work," Twyla said, pointing to the cutters. They were almost all women or girls in their teens. There were a few young boys. "They's almost a rhythm to the way they move. See? Reach into a lug box. Pick up a 'cot. Stick that short knife aginst it. Twist. Take out the pit from the two halves. Drop the pit inta one box and the two halves o' fruit onta the tray." She grinned, proud of her observations.

They continued to watch. When a lug was emptied, the cutters raised their voices. "Fruit!" they called. Or if it was a Mexican cutter, she would call out, "Fruta!" rolling her r's. In either case, men brought full boxes of apricots and placed them in front of the person who had called out. Since a cutter was paid by the lug, each worked rapidly.

Hildy and Twyla walked out into the sunlight as men loaded the full trays onto small carts. These were pushed along narrow tracks toward the small sheds where sulphur fumes rose into the morning air.

The girls continued toward town, and a short way down the road Twyla pointed. "Yonder's the sign I saw 'bout pickers wanted. If'n we had on boys' clothes, I reckon we might git us a job."

Hildy watched the crews moving into the orchards with their picking buckets and ladders. Suddenly Hildy nudged Twyla. "Look! Isn't that Don Gridley talking to those pickers in the first row?"

"Ain't nobody else but him. Let's walk right on by real fast an' maybe he won't see us and start trouble."

Hildy shook her head. "No, you go on, but I've got to talk to him."

"Ye tetched in the haid, Hildy?"

"I've got to ask him about my father's watch."

Twyla's eyes grew wide. "Air ye gonna accuse him of stealin' that thar watch?"

"No, I'm going to give him a chance to save face while I make it plain that I'm onto him."

"Maybe he didn't really swipe it."

"Had to be him. Wait for me down the road."

Twyla moaned. "No, if yore bound and d'termined to do it, I'll walk up with ye."

Hildy waited until the half-dozen pickers around had taken their ladders into the rows of trees and were too far away to overhear.

Don Gridley turned as the girls approached. "What do you two want?" he demanded, shifting his cowboy hat to the back of his head.

Hildy swallowed hard. "If you've got my father's watch, I'd appreciate it if you'd return it."

The boy frowned fiercely. "I don't know what you're talking about," he snapped. "But if you're suggesting that I stole something from your old man, you're crazier than I thought."

Hildy had a sudden, terrible feeling that she shouldn't have said anything. Still, she was committed, and she couldn't back down now. "It was my great-grandfather's, and it means the world to my daddy," she said softly.

For a moment, Don stared at her, his mouth working but no words coming out. Abruptly, he raised his right hand and pointed toward the road. "Get off of my property!" he shouted. "And stay out of my sight, or you'll be sorry!"

As the girls hurried toward the road, Twyla muttered, "I tol' ye not to do that!"

"I know! I know!"

"Well, they's no use cryin' over spilt milk, Hildy. Ye done what ye done, and that's that. Only I'd practically g'arantee that ye ain't heerd the last of this."

At the post office, the girls asked if anyone had been inquiring about them. The clerk shook his head. "Nope, not yet. But sooner or later, everybody shows up here asking for somebody. You want to leave a message, girls?"

Hildy hesitated a moment. "We're expecting a boy named Spud, so when he comes—"

"Spud?" the clerk said with a knowing smile. "Oh, I remember his letter now. He your boyfriend?"

Suddenly Hildy felt flustered. "No! Oh, no! He's just a boy who loaned me his dictionary, and he's coming to get it."

The man behind the grillwork chuckled. "Well, now, that's a good one. Now, if you'll give me a description of this Spud and leave your message, I'll see that he gets it," he said with a wink.

Still somewhat embarrassed, Hildy managed to tell the postmaster about the tents by the bridge. "If the blue one's not there," she added, "tell him we're at the barn-house on the old Wood Brothers property."

As the girls walked out of town and back to the bridge, they talked the whole way. Then crossing to the far end of the bridge, where the steep, narrow dirt trail wound down to the tents, they heard a loud noise and turned around. An old Model T Ford came out from town and crossed behind them. Steam poured from the radiator.

"Hey, girls!" the male driver called.

The girls stared at the man alone in the car. He wore grimy overalls, a slouch hat, and a blue shirt buttoned at the neck and sleeves. He hadn't shaved in a long time.

The man pulled up beside the girls and stuck his head out of the open driver's side. "This here the place that's got a passel of kids to give away?"

Twyla drew a sharp breath, obviously remembering her parents' conversation earlier in the week. She clamped her hand on Hildy's wrist so tightly that it hurt.

Hildy stalled. "What's that?"

The man gestured impatiently. "Guess ye don't know nothin' 'bout it. I need me some hands to work the chicken

ranch, and I thought . . . Oh, well, maybe it's the next bridge."
He pulled away, leaving the girls standing in stunned silence.

Hildy watched the car round a curve before she turned to
look at her friend.

Twyla's face was white and her eyes were glistening with
tears. "So that's where Pop went this mornin'."

"Now, Twyla, you don't know that. So don't go getting yourself all upset."

"It's come to that!" Twyla cried, clamping both hands to her
face in shocked disbelief. "It's a-happenin', Hildy!"

"It'll work out, Twyla." Hildy put her arms around her
friend's trembling body and pulled her close. "It'll be okay."

"No, it won't. That's why my folks was a-whisperin' in the
night. And that's why Mama was a-cryin' when Pop drove off
this mornin'. Oh, Hildy, what'm I gonna do?"

"We'll think of something. Now, get hold of yourself, and
let's go down to the camp and try to think."

It took several minutes for Twyla to regain her composure.
Then the girls slid on their backsides down the steep, narrow
path that led to the tents. As they approached, they saw no one.
That meant everyone was still at the brush arbor.

Then Hildy heard the sound of a file on metal. She stopped,
looking at her friend.

Twyla's face clouded. "Pop's back," she whispered. "Oh,
Hildy, I cain't look at 'im. I'd bust out cryin'."

"What're you going to do?"

"I don't know, maybe walk down by the river a spell. Ye go
ahead into the camp if'n ye want, and I'll come in when'st I feel
better."

"I don't want to leave you . . ."

"Go on. Please. I gotta be alone to think."

Hildy reluctantly went on by herself, realizing that the
Depression meant more than just hard times for people without
money or jobs. It meant people suffering in the worst way.

Suddenly Twyla turned back and grabbed Hildy's arm.
"Wait! I know what we kin do."

"What?"

"Let's put on some of my brothers' clothes and go back to see if we kin git a job pickin' cots."

Hildy started to protest, but then she saw the terrible fear and pain in Twyla's eyes. "Well," Hildy said uncertainly.

"Look, I'm desper't! Ye want to have me'n all my brothers an' sisters give' to strangers like that one on the bridge?"

"Of course not."

"Then let's do it."

Hildy took a slow breath and nodded. "I just hope Don Gridley doesn't find out."

"It's better'n bein' give' away like a passel of puppies."

Tears filled Hildy's eyes. "Let's get started," she said.

CHAPTER FIFTEEN

TREETOP THOUGHTS

When Hildy and Twyla walked back into the orchard, Don Gridley was nowhere in sight. The girls were dressed in boys' overalls and blue work shirts, their hair tucked under men's hats. Finding the foreman, a dark, swarthy man with a red handkerchief around his neck, the disguised girls said they wanted to work as pickers.

He studied them through dark, hard eyes. "You both look too puny to handle a ladder in these trees," he said at last. "But I'm short-handed, and the fruit's going to rot if I don't get it picked fast. Okay, grab a bucket and get busy!"

Hildy was surprised how hard a twelve-foot ladder was to move through an orchard. With difficulty, she managed to drag it from tree to tree, climb with her bucket, and pick the small yellow fruit with a rosy blush to its downy skin. The tree limbs kept knocking Hildy's hat around, threatening to expose her long brown braids carefully tied on top of her head.

After a while, Hildy called softly, "How you doing, Twyla?"

Her friend didn't answer.

Alarmed, Hildy leaned against the ladder and pushed the

dark green leaves apart to see into the next row. Twyla's arms were moving swiftly, her fingers flitting from one apricot to another in a frantic rush, picking three or four fruits at the same time.

What would it be like if my sisters were given away to strangers? Hildy wondered. She shivered in spite of the hot sun beating down on them in the orchard.

As she continued picking, she noticed a mourning dove's sad cooing song in the distance. Nearby, honey bees and wasps buzzed away in search of their own treasure. They all seemed to be enjoying themselves, but this was hard work. Hildy wished it weren't so important to Twyla.

During the next hour's work, she fidgeted uncomfortably, the dust thick on her legs where it drifted up the legs of her borrowed overalls. Dust also clogged her nostrils and caked her throat. She looked around for some hope of relief. Spying a brown jug of water wrapped in a wet burlap sack resting against a tree trunk, Hildy decided to go down the ladder for a drink.

As she reached for one last apricot to fill her bucket before starting down, her hand closed on something strange. Before she could open her hand, a sharp pain stabbed her right forefinger. "Ouch!" she cried, popping the stung finger into her mouth. "That hurt!" A honey bee quickly flew away, and Hildy shook her finger instinctively. The ladder swayed and she almost fell. But finally she managed to regain her balance and examine the finger. It was already red and starting to swell.

"That does it!" she shouted, almost sobbing with pain. "I'm not cut out to pick fruit." Hurrying down the ladder, nursing her throbbing finger, she emptied her bucket into a lug box between the rows of trees and ran over to Twyla's ladder.

"I quit!" Hildy cried, looking up to where her friend was still picking fast. "I'm going to get an education and never again be a cotton picker, or apricot picker, or anything else!"

Twyla looked down with the saddest eyes Hildy had ever seen, but the flying hands did not stop. "I'm sorry you got hurt, Hildy. I got into some wasps a few minutes back and they stung me purty good."

For the first time, Hildy saw the puffy red welts on Twyla's face and forehead. "Oh." Hildy frowned with concern. "I'm so sorry."

"It's okay," Twyla said. "It's fer my brothers an' sisters, so it don't hurt so bad."

Ashamed of her own selfishness, Hildy turned back to her row. With new determination, she snatched up her bucket and climbed the ladder again.

Before, she hadn't paid much attention to her friend's brothers and sisters. Now she tried to make them as real to herself as they were to Twyla. Their names and faces paraded through her mind.

Five girls and four boys! she thought in wonder. *They're all going to be given away unless* . . . Hildy shook her head, refusing to let that terrible thought remain in her mind.

As sundown approached, the foreman came by and called the pickers down from their ladders. He paid each in cash for the number of boxes they had filled.

Hildy had earned her first money picking cotton when she was seven years old. Now, at twelve, she was picking apricots, yet for all her hard work she had earned only sixty cents. It was discouraging, but at least the coins would help.

Twyla had earned a silver dollar, which she clutched in her swollen, bleeding hands. The wasp stings had made large, ugly blotches on her face, but she ignored the pain.

The bone-weary, unhappy girls walked in silence until they reached the bridge. Then they made their way across and slid down the steep embankment.

At the river's edge, Twyla finally spoke. "May's well skin outta these dirty clothes and wash up some in the river before we get to the tents."

Hildy looked around and decided that no one could see in the gathering dusk. Dropping the boys' overalls, she gazed at her legs in disbelief. They were literally caked with dust and itched painfully.

The girls eased into the shallow water behind some thick

young willows. "When this is over," Hildy said, "I'm never again going to pick fruit. Depression or not, I'm going to find something else to do to help buy the kids' school clothes."

Twyla washed vigorously in the cold water. "I got me no choice. I'm gonna he'p Pop all's I kin so's he don't have to give us kids away."

Hildy was so tired she started to cry, her tears flowing more out of concern for her friend than from her own exhaustion. "I hate this Depression," she whispered angrily into the nearly dark sky. "I hate it. Hate it!"

When the girls parted at the camps, Hildy wondered what would happen at the Hockett tent that night. Would Twyla's parents tell the kids they were going to be given away?

Hildy decided not to say anything about the situation to her father or stepmother unless they mentioned it. If they didn't, that meant Mrs. Hockett hadn't told Molly. It also meant nobody else had been around inquiring about swapping food for kids.

Just outside the tent in the pale light of the coal oil lamp, Hildy's father and stepmother greeted her with concern. "Hildy," her father said sternly, "you know you're supposed to be home before dark. Where have you been? And why are you wearing those old overalls?"

Hildy dug into the bib pocket and produced the coins. "Picking 'cots," she said, briefly explaining what she and Twyla had done. She held out the coins to her father. "Here. This is to help buy school clothes for the kids."

Her father shook his head and pushed the outstretched hand away. "It's not your place to provide for this family, Hildy! I'll take care of us. All of us."

"I was just trying to help, Daddy."

Molly shook her head slowly. "Seems to me that wearing those boys' clothes is kind of like a lie. Don't you think so, Hildy?"

"We didn't say we were boys."

"Would they have hired you if they knew you were girls?" Molly asked.

Hildy just stood there, not knowing what to say. She had expected praise for having brought home some money, so she was surprised at this reaction. Tired and sick at heart, she spun around and walked away without saying anything more.

After a little while, Hildy helped bathe her sisters in a pan of water heated over the open fire; then she helped put them to bed. But she was so weary that she didn't talk much. And she sank wearily onto her pallet long before her usual bedtime.

The next morning when she awoke, stiff and sore, she heard her father's angry voice again. "I tell you, Molly, it's gone! Just like my watch."

Hildy forced her protesting body to an upright position. "What's gone?"

"My safety razor. It was right on the stump outside the tent where I always leave it."

Hildy remembered Don Gridley's furious reaction when she suggested that he might have stolen her father's gold watch. The watch had value, but a razor only cost a few cents.

Suddenly, Hildy remembered something. "Daddy, could it have been a trade rat?"

"A what?"

"You know, those rats that take something to their nests but always leave something in it's . . . ?" Her voice trailed off. The day before there had been nothing left in place of the watch. And from the look on her father's face, there was none this morning, either.

Joe Corrigan shook his head angrily. "No pack rat took my razor or my watch." He frowned thoughtfully and added, "But maybe it *was* some kind of an animal."

Father and daughter went outside to check for animal tracks. There were none.

Hildy ventured a slight smile. "If we had a pet dog, he wouldn't let anybody or anything steal from us," she said wistfully.

"Now, Hildy," her father muttered, "you know we got no way of feeding a dog."

"Still, I wish we had a pet." Just then Hildy heard footsteps outside and peeked out to see Twyla walking out of the other tent. Hildy was startled at her friend's appearance. Twyla wore overalls and a blue shirt buttoned at the neck and wrists. She had shoes on her feet, but she walked stiffly, staring straight ahead as though not seeing Hildy.

Hildy slipped into her dress and ran out to meet her. "You all right?" she asked.

"Oh, Hildy!" Twyla's voice was so full of sadness and pain that Hildy stopped in her tracks. "Oh, Hildy!" The words rose in a pained shriek, and Twyla doubled over in sobs.

Molly came running out of the blue tent with the baby in her arms and motioned Hildy to get Twyla inside. Seconds later Twyla collapsed on the upturned lug box, sobbing her heart out.

Hildy briefly explained to Molly about the man on the bridge. "I guess Twyla's folks told her this morning."

Slowly Twyla raised her head. Her face was still swollen from the previous day's wasp stings, and her eyes were wet with tears. "Oh, I cain't believe it," she moaned. "Pop says yestiddy he went back to all the agencies that're supposed to he'p people, but nobody'll do anythin'."

She sniffed and went on. "So this mornin' my folks tol' us kids they got no choice. In order fer us to survive, they got to . . . to . . . give us away!" She sobbed uncontrollably.

Hildy knelt beside her friend and hugged her tight, rocking back and forth, not knowing what to say. Hildy heard her parents talking softly to each other but couldn't understand what they were saying. All the Corrigan children had awakened but sat silently on their pallets, aware that something terrible was going on.

When Twyla's body stopped shaking from the convulsive sobs, she raised her eyes and looked around the tent at each member of the Corrigan family. "Oh, what'm I going to do? I'll die if'n my family is separated!"

Hildy had never felt so helpless. Reaching under her pillow, she pulled out the coins she had earned picking apricots.

"Here," she said, pressing them into her friend's hand. "It's not much, but . . ." Her voice trailed off then, and she looked imploringly at her father and stepmother.

Joe Corrigan sighed deeply. "We'll try to think of some way to help," he promised.

After he had left for work and Twyla had gone back to her tent to be alone with her family, Hildy, in hushed tones, explained to her little sisters what was happening in the Hocketts' tent.

Molly's face showed deep concern. "I've been secretly sharing what little we had," she said, "especially milk for baby Kallie, but I had no idea they were so desperate."

That was one of the most lonely, sad, miserable days of Hildy's life. She wanted to be with her friend, but Twyla came over only briefly to say that her parents wanted her to stay close. People would be coming to choose children.

Hildy sadly watched Twyla return to her tent; then she heard crying from that direction. Hildy couldn't stand it. She asked Molly if she could take the kids and go play with them in the flat, open area near the brush arbor.

While her sisters played kick the can, fox and geese, burn base, and other games, Hildy walked into the brush arbor and sat down. No one else was around.

The cool morning breeze had died, and the dry leaves on the roof became silent. The mourning doves quit calling in the distance, and the smell of dust from the brush arbor floor came faintly to Hildy's nostrils.

"Why, Lord?" Hildy whispered, looking up. "Why does this terrible Depression go on so long? Why do nice people like the Hocketts have to suffer so much?"

Then a thought came, unwelcome but persistent. Hildy remembered her grandfather's words. "How people look at life makes a big difference," he had said.

Hildy pondered that. How did her father and Twyla's father look at life differently? Hildy didn't know, but she realized that her father had repeatedly gone out looking for work while Mr. Hockett had not.

Hildy's father had come home with liquor on his breath a couple of times but not since he landed a job. Had Mr. Hockett given up? Hildy didn't know, and she certainly couldn't discuss that with Twyla.

Suddenly a big Packard car stopped beside the brush arbor, the tires leaving a rooster tail of dust. Inside, there was a nicely dressed middle-aged man and woman. The man leaned out and called to Hildy. "Say, young lady, do you know how to get to those tents by the bridge?"

As Hildy got up from the crude log bench and walked over to the car, her sisters came running up to see what was going on. The Hocketts' situation was so heavy on her mind that without thinking, Hildy gave him directions.

The couple politely thanked Hildy and drove away.

Elizabeth looked at Hildy. "Wonder which one of the Hockett kids they want?" she said.

"Oh no!" Hildy exclaimed in horror. "Oh my, I didn't think—" She turned and fled back into the brush arbor. *Oh, Lord*, she prayed silently, *please don't let it be Twyla! . . . I've got to get home!*

Hildy hurried her sisters toward the camp. At the edge of the flat, open area, Hildy peered anxiously down into the river bottom, terrified of what she would see.

CHAPTER SIXTEEN

A SAD GOODBYE

Hildy and her sisters ran down the riverbank and across the grassy area toward the two tents near the bridge. Hildy's chest felt tight, as though someone had thrown a rope around it and was pulling hard. She could barely breathe as she strained to see or hear something from the silent camp.

As they entered the bridge's shadow, Hildy couldn't stand the suspense any longer. While still running, she cupped her hands to her mouth to call. "Twyla! Twyla, are you there?"

There was no answer, no sound from the dusty white tent.

A moment later Molly pushed the flap open on the second tent. "The Hocketts aren't here!" she called, balancing baby Joey on her hip.

"Where'd they go?"

"I don't know," Molly replied as Hildy and the girls reached the tent. "Some strangers came, saying they wanted to look at the children they'd heard about. Mr. Hockett went out to talk to them, but Twyla, her brothers and sisters set up such a howl that Mr. Hockett sent the people away."

Molly shifted Joey to the other hip. "A few minutes later, the whole Hockett family got in their old car and drove away. Didn't say where they were going. Just left real fast."

For a moment Hildy felt relieved. Then another fear seized her. Where *had* the Hocketts gone and when would they come back?

Suddenly Martha let out a yell. "Hey, lookee! Daddy's coming!"

Molly shaded her eyes to look across the shallow river. "Wonder why he's coming home this time of day?" she mused aloud. "Oh, I hope he hasn't lost his job."

As Joe Corrigan eased the touring car out of the river and onto the bank, the whole family swarmed around him. Hildy was first to notice that his left cheek was swollen and turning an ugly mixture of red and purple.

"Daddy, what happened?" she cried as he got out of the car.

"Oh, it's nothing much. Some fellow took a swing at me when I got a night job he wanted as grammar school janitor. The guy claimed it wasn't right for me to have two jobs when he didn't have any.

"I tried to explain that I got this job because I needed it badly. My boss, Mr. Wood, had recommended me to the school principal because I was a hard worker."

"Oh, Daddy," Hildy said, lightly touching his face, "I'm sorry you got hurt."

He shrugged. "It'll be okay. Anyway, now you'll have school clothes because I'm going to be the night janitor at Lone River Grammar School, starting tonight. So Mr. Wood gave me a couple hours off to get moved."

"Moved?" All five girls echoed the word together.

Their father nodded. "Right now. I'll be working sixteen hours a day, so we've got to move to the barn-house while we can."

"We can't do that now," Hildy protested, pointing to the Hocketts' tent. "We don't know what happened to Twyla and her family."

Briefly, Molly explained to her husband what had been going on.

Joe Corrigan shook his head. "I'm sorry, but we've got no choice but to move—now. However, if you all agree, we'll postpone buying school clothes for a while and use the extra money to help the Hocketts."

A happy chorus went up, but Joe Corrigan cut it short. "Okay, okay. We've got no time to lose. Let's start packing fast."

The ever-practical Elizabeth objected. "What about the rotten egg smell at the barn-house?"

"We'll just have to put up with it, girls. Now, grab your things and get them into the car."

Hildy didn't want to leave until she knew what had happened to Twyla, but her father was in no mood for unnecessary delays. Reluctantly, Hildy helped pack the car with pots, pans, and personal belongings. As she set another box onto the running board, Martha called out from the far side of the car.

"Hey, Daddy, you've got a puncture!"

The whole family quickly gathered around the flat left rear tire.

Joe Corrigan kicked the tire. "Must've picked up a nail," he grumbled. "By the time I patch that, we won't have time to move everything. I'll have to come back later."

Hildy felt a surge of hope. *Then I'll get to see Twyla again*, she thought.

Hildy's father stroked his chin. "Leave the beds and the tent so we can sleep here again tonight," he said. "We'll finish moving at first light tomorrow before I leave for the Woods' ranch."

Hildy watched vainly, hoping the Hocketts would return before the tire was fixed. But there was no sign of Twyla and her family when the Corrigan car, fully loaded with everything else, left the river camp and turned toward the barn-house.

As they approached it, Hildy stuck her head out of the car and sniffed. "Still smells terrible!" she announced.

Her father shrugged. "Can't help it," he said in resignation. "But the eggs are all on the east side, so I'll park at the west end and unload. Just stick things inside the door for now."

Getting out of the car, he pushed the northwestern sliding

door open. "I'll barely get all of you back to the tent and me to the ranch before my couple hours are up. So hurry. I can't afford to lose either of my jobs."

Everyone else was anxious to see the inside of the barn-house where they were to live, but Mr. Corrigan only wanted to unload quickly. In a few minutes, the last box was deposited inside the barn.

As he closed the barn door, he stopped, looking at the dry grass growing right up against the western wall. "Molly," he said, "remind me to cut that back first chance I get. It's dry as tinder. If it caught on fire, the flames would go right up the wall, and we'd lose the whole place."

All of a sudden Hildy thought of something. "Wait!" she exclaimed. "I'll be right back." Without explaining, she ran off toward the long tangle of blackberry patches.

She returned a few minutes later, puffing hard, carrying the box trap she and Twyla had found earlier. "Look, Daddy," she said, "if an animal took your watch and razor, maybe we can catch it tonight."

"Maybe," he agreed, putting the trap on the running board. "Everyone get in now. We've got to hurry."

As the car cleared the cottonwoods and willows on the western river bank, Hildy leaned forward anxiously. She peered eagerly through the windshield. "There she is!" Hildy cried, pointing across the river. "Twyla's back. They're all back."

When the car stopped on the eastern shore, Hildy jumped out and ran to her friend. "Where did you go? I was worried sick."

Twyla's eyes were red and her cheeks, still swollen from the wasp stings, were streaked with dried tears. "Our pop took us all down to the county offices so they could see the bunch of us. He said it was one last time to make them see what we're up against, but . . ." Her voice trailed off.

Hildy clutched her friend's hands in hers. "What happened?"

"Nothin'." Twyla sniffed and wiped the back of her hand

across her eyes. "They said they cain't he'p, so . . . so . . . to-morry Pop says we gotta do it."

Hildy didn't ask what that meant. She knew. Trying to cheer her friend, she changed the subject. "We're moving tomorrow, but tonight maybe we can catch that animal that stole Daddy's things. I brought that box trap we saw at the barn-house. Where do you think we should set it?"

Twyla didn't seem to be in the mood for such trivial things, but she agreed to help set the trap, seeming anxious for a chance to talk to Hildy privately. As the girls chose a spot within two feet of the blue tent's flap, Hildy ached at the thought of her friend's terrible future.

"Let's use both food and something shiny," Hildy suggested. "In case it is an animal, two baits would be better than one."

"How about a fish head?" Twyla asked.

"I hate the smell, but an animal might like it," Hildy admitted. "Oh, and I've got a new Indian Head penny from yesterday. That's bright and shiny."

That night, the two friends stayed up as long as they could. They said they were watching the trap, but they really were reluctant to part. They knew it might be their last evening together. Finally, with a tearful hug, they separated and went to their own tents.

In the middle of the night Hildy awakened to a growling, squealing, banging sound. She sat up on her pallet in the darkness.

Her father's voice called out through the night. "What's that racket? Molly, where's the lamp?"

Hildy trembled in fear. "What is it, Daddy?"

"Your trap, I think. Sounds like you caught something."

Her father lit the lamp, and Hildy saw that her sisters were all awake. Soon their sleepy voices were asking a dozen anxious questions. Baby Joey also awoke with a screech, and Molly tried to calm him while the others followed their father and the lamp through the tent flap and into the night.

Hildy saw right away that the trap was sprung. The wooden

door had snapped down and locked. She ran behind her father to the other end of the two-foot-long trap, where the wire mesh was.

Mr. Corrigan bent and held the light up to see through the wire into the trap. A pair of glowing eyes reflected the lamp's light, and a low, warning growl came from the box.

Hildy looked up. "What is it, Daddy?"

Her father began to chuckle. "There's our burglar—mask and everything."

Hildy recognized it then. "A young raccoon! Oh, Daddy, it's so cute. Can we keep it?"

Hildy's sisters began begging in chorus, "Can we, Daddy? Please?"

Just then the Hocketts came rushing out of their tent to see what was happening, and they all stood around, gazing at the frightened little animal.

Elizabeth nudged her father. "You said we could have a pet," she reminded him, "so can we keep this little fella?"

"We'll decide that in the morning, girls. Meanwhile, Mr. 'Coon can stay right there until we figure out what to do with him. He won't steal anything, and he won't get hurt as long as he's in the trap."

The younger Corrigan girls talked about the raccoon for a long time until they finally fell asleep, but Hildy's mind turned again to Twyla.

Just before dawn, Hildy awakened when she heard her father crawl out of the pallet he shared with Molly and the baby.

"Daddy," Hildy whispered, "may I stay with Twyla today, please?"

"I know how you feel," he whispered above the other children's light snoring, "but Molly'll need you to help watch the kids and get settled in the barn-house."

"Please, Daddy? Just for a while?"

He looked at her for a long moment in thoughtful silence. "Well, I'll ask Molly. If she can spare you for a couple of hours, it's okay. But then you'd have to walk to the barn-house."

"I'll run there if you'll just let me stay awhile," Hildy promised.

Elizabeth sat up suddenly. "Daddy, can we keep the raccoon?"

He reached over and ruffled her tousled, light blond hair. "Molly and I talked about that after you kids went back to sleep," he said. "The 'coon's big enough to be weaned, and I've known folks who had 'coons for pets. They make good ones, I hear. So I guess it's okay on the condition you kids feed him from something besides what little we've got for ourselves."

"H'rayyyyy!" Elizabeth cried, jolting Martha, Sarah, and Iola out of their sound sleep.

"Shhh!" their father warned. "You'll wake the baby."

Since it wasn't quite light enough outside to see, he lit the coal oil lamp. "I've been thinking," he said. "Since this is a young 'coon, there must be a hollow tree around close by. If we can find it, maybe I can recover my watch before we move."

"We'll look for it," Hildy offered. As she scrambled out of bed, her sisters tumbling after her, they slipped into their clothes.

Mr. Corrigan carried the lamp as the girls raced toward the nearest tree.

Twyla came out of her tent and joined them. "I been a-hearin' a kind of chirring noise the last couple of nights," she said. "Reckon that had to be made by raccoons. Seemed to be a-comin' from that tree right over yonder."

The moment the light hit the hole high up in an old cottonwood with the top broken off, a pair of eyes reflected back.

"Another 'coon!" Hildy cried. "Daddy, look!"

"I see it." Taking the lamp closer, he examined the hole. By then the second raccoon had vanished into the hollow top, but Mr. Corrigan was satisfied. "That's our nest tree all right. It's an old one, so I'll get the ax and chop it down as soon as it's light enough."

"Maybe my pop could he'p with his saw," Twyla offered.

"I'd be obliged," Hildy's father replied.

Dawn came fast, and soon Mr. Hockett came out of his tent with what he called a *Swede fiddle*, a two-man saw. It took the two men only a few minutes to bring the old tree crashing down, and the minute the top hit the ground, a full-grown racoon bounded out and vanished into the morning light.

Mr. Corrigan used his ax to chop around the hole, then shined the lamp inside. "There's my watch!" he cried, reaching inside. "And my razor, and no telling what all these other things are."

For a moment Hildy felt excited; then sadness covered her. She looked at Twyla. Neither spoke. They both understood the awful thing that would happen that day. And even the Corrigans' offer of financial assistance wasn't enough to prevent it.

A few minutes later the rest of the Corrigans' belongings were loaded onto the Lexington, and Hildy took one last look around. Where the blue tent had stood, there was now only flattened bermuda grass. The long, one-piece center tent pole was lashed into place on the car's roof. The pole stuck out over the hood and back over the spare tire. On the left running board, the box trap with its masked occupant rested securely beside pots and pans.

The time had come to say goodbye.

The adults shook hands with each other and said soft words while Hildy's sisters did the same with the Hockett children. But Hildy and Twyla walked side by side toward the river to be alone one last moment.

"Well," Twyla said as she stared across the water barely glistening with the morning's first sunlight, "reckon we won't be a-seein' each other no more, Hildy."

"Don't say that. We'll see each other. Lots of times. And you'll meet Spud someday, too."

Twyla shook her head. "I hope so, but 'tain't likely." Her voice was sad and barely audible. "My pop says a couple is comin' back to look at me—nice-lookin' man and woman in a big Packard."

Hildy's head jerked up suddenly. *The same ones I sent here!*

she thought. *I did it. They'll come and take Twyla away, and I won't see her again.*

Aloud, Hildy tried to sound hopeful. "Maybe it won't happen."

"Maybe," Twyla agreed. "But if it does, I don't keer whether I live or die, never to see my family agin, never to see ye—" Her voice broke.

Reaching out, Hildy pulled Twyla close, and they cried together, lost in helplessness.

CHAPTER SEVENTEEN

WHEN NOBODY UNDERSTANDS

Hildy opened her eyes and looked up as her father cleared his throat. "Sorry, Hildy," he said softly. "Time to go."

Hildy reluctantly released Twyla and fingered her long brown braids. "Did you ask Molly if I could stay awhile longer?"

Her father nodded. "She needs you now."

Hildy's teary blue eyes turned toward the Lexington. Her stepmother was holding the baby in her arms and carefully stepping over the packed running board to get into the car. The other four Corrigan kids were already in the backseat.

Hildy looked at Molly, silently begging for permission.

Molly hesitated, then closed the car door. "Hildy, I can spare you an hour, no more," she called.

Hildy gave a glad cry. "Thanks," she called back. Then she hugged Twyla again. They were still holding each other in a silent embrace when Hildy's father eased the Lexington Minuteman into the shallow river and headed for the western shore.

A moment later Twyla's mother called to her. The girl

sniffed, reluctantly broke the embrace, and dried her eyes. "I got to he'p in the tent," she said. "You want t' come along?"

Hildy nodded, still too choked up to speak. As the two friends turned toward the tent, Hildy heard the anguished cries inside and realized how much each of the Hockett children was suffering.

Before the girls reached the tent, an old Model T Ford stopped on the bridge overhead. Hildy glanced up. Instantly she recognized the man with grimy overalls, slouch hat, and blue shirt. He was the one who had first asked if this was the place that had kids to give away.

"Hey!" The driver stuck his head out of the car and waved. "Hey, gals, where's your pappy?"

The girls glanced at each other, remembering the man. He hadn't changed clothes or shaved.

Just then Twyla's father came out of the tent. He seemed thinner than ever, and his shoulders slumped more. He looked up at the stranger on the bridge. "Are ye a-lookin' fer me, Mister?"

"You got a passel of kids to give away?"

Mr. Hockett groaned. "Drive to the west side of the bridge—" His voice broke as he called out to the man. "—and come down that dirt road." He motioned toward the other side of the river. "It's shallow. Ye kin cross there."

Twyla choked back a sob and dashed toward the tent. Hildy did not follow. She sensed that Twyla needed to be with her family in this terrible time of separation. Hildy was a friend, but she was not family.

Inside the tent, the wailing grew louder, piercing the dusty canvas walls. The Hockett kids and their mother must have heard the man's call from the bridge.

Hildy turned blindly away. Staggering back to where the blue tent had stood, she threw herself across the dried boughs that had been her bedding and sobbed hard.

It's not real, she tried to tell herself a few minutes later. *It's not happening!*

But it was real and it was happening. She sat up when she

heard the steaming radiator of the Model T as it pulled out of the shallow river and stopped beside the Hockett tent.

"Oh, Lord," she whispered, "please, not to that man."

Hildy couldn't bear to watch. She buried her head in her hands and heard the low murmur of the men's voices. A moment later, Mr. Hockett called his older sons. His voice was sad and soft. "Burl and Ferris, you boys come out hyar."

Hildy still couldn't look. Sick at heart, she lay face down on the boughs, feeling a terrible ache throughout her body. Next, she heard the Hockett boys' voices and the chicken rancher saying something about a box of groceries.

Then came the sound of the man cranking the Model T, followed by a high-pitched, bitter cry, so sharp and full of agony that Hildy spun around and looked.

The grimy man slid under the wheel, and turned the car toward the river. Fifteen-year-old Ferris sat glumly in the backseat, but his younger brother thrust out both hands and screamed, "No! No! Pop, don't let 'im! Mama! Oh, Mama! Nooooo!"

Hildy couldn't stand it. Jumping up, she ran blindly toward the river, her hands over her ears, long brown braids flying behind. But she could still hear the boy's final, terrible scream as the car entered the water. Then there was only the sobbing and wailing of his parents and the brothers and sisters in the white tent.

Hildy collapsed with a painful stitch in her side. As she lay on a small patch of brown sand at the river's edge, she tried to pray, but the words wouldn't come.

Then she heard another car crossing the river, and she knew the same tragic scene would be repeated.

Hildy tried not to listen, but soon there was again the murmur of strange voices, a mention of food, and the sound of a car starting up again. Hildy glanced up, fearful it was Twyla being taken away.

Hildy blinked at the brightness of the sunshine. It wasn't right for the sun to be shining so gloriously when her friends were suffering in such black despair.

There was a Dodge leaving through the shallow water now, and in the backseat, ten-year-old Charley and four-year-old Abner were screaming, reaching out imploring hands to their parents.

Hildy spun around, trying to blot out the pitiful sight. She knew the boys would go first because they could, or soon would be able to work in the fields and orchards. Girls were less desirable because they ate but couldn't produce as much.

Still, there were strangers who wanted girls, too. One by one, the cars left with screaming Hockett children.

But none of them was Twyla.

Hildy guessed her hour was about up. She would have to leave. Her insides were churning, and her face felt stiff with dried, salty tears, but Hildy got up slowly from the patch of sand by the river.

She tried to blot out the memory of those soul-wrenching cries, yet she knew she would never forget, not really. Those cries would echo in her mind for years to come.

Outside the old Hockett tent, Hildy heard the muffled sobs within. Reluctantly, she raised her voice. "Twyla, I've got to go now."

Twyla pushed through the flap. She looked terrible. The swelling from the wasp stings and hours of anguished crying made Twyla's face red and puffy.

"Oh, Hildy!" Twyla moaned, desperately crushing her friend in her arms. "Oh, Hildy, I'll never, never see 'em agin!"

Hildy tried to comfort her friend with soft words and loving pats, but she soon heard another car approaching. Both girls raised their eyes.

The Packard with the nice-looking couple Hildy had seen at the brush arbor was easing into the shallow river crossing.

Twyla turned her head back to face Hildy, her eyes wide with fear. "Oh, Hildy, it's them! The same ones that come before. They's a-comin' to git me."

Hildy couldn't leave now, not even if being late would upset Molly. She stood back helplessly while the couple from the big Packard talked with Twyla's parents. Hildy caught the word, *adopt*. She hadn't heard that said before.

Numbly, Hildy watched as Twyla kissed her remaining sisters and her parents.

Then Twyla ran to Hildy for a final hug. "Oh, Hildy," Twyla moaned into the brown braids, "ye been the best friend I ever had."

Hildy was so numb with pain she didn't remember what she said in reply. But soon the nice-looking couple in the luxury sedan left, taking Twyla with them.

Hildy wanted to run after them, screaming, *No! No! You can't take her*! Instead, she stumbled wordlessly down the riverbank. The anguished cries of Twyla's family followed her.

As she had before, she ran blindly, ignoring the willow branches stinging her arms and face. Through hot, blurring tears, she saw only the river—dark, deep, and swift.

She ran and ran until she collapsed, exhausted, against the trunk of an old cottonwood. For a long time, Hildy's body shook with great, racking sobs. Then, when all her tears were gone and she felt dry and empty, she raised her eyes to the clear, cloudless sky. "Why?" she whispered fiercely. "Why? Why? Why?"

She waited, listening for some answer. But she heard only the river, sliding contentedly by, serene and purposeful.

Hildy looked up and wiped her eyes. A light breeze touched the cottonwoods' leaves, and they trembled softly, as though also suffering.

Hildy had a sudden, terrible urge to shake her fist at the pretty blue sky and blame God. It was all so unfair.

Then, more weak and weary than she could remember, except when her mother died, Hildy lay down on the riverbank between two exposed tree roots. She looked up but her eyes did not focus.

She didn't know how long she lay there drained of everything except pain. Her mind felt numb. How could so much misery smash her small world?

Suddenly a thought struck her. *What was it Grandma and Granddad Corrigan said?* Hildy couldn't remember the exact words, but it was something like, "Some things in life can't be explained or understood. When that happens, all you can do is trust."

Hildy forced her numb mind to recall the verse her grand-parents had told her about and underlined in the small Bible they had given her. Hildy had found the verse in Proverbs when she was reading one night before bed, and she quickly memo-rized it.

Trust in the Lord with all thine heart; and lean not unto thine own understanding. In all thy ways acknowledge him. . . . Hildy shook her head, her braids flying, as other thoughts flooded her mind.

There's no way I can ever understand what happened to the Hock-etts, she thought. *They're good people, yet they'll probably never be together as a family again. But you're blessed, Hildy Corrigan. You and your family are together now, and they're going to stay that way.*

Hildy suddenly felt ashamed of her reaction to the barn-house they would soon be living in. *You want a "forever home," but what would it be like without your father, Molly, Elizabeth, Mar-tha, Sarah, Iola, and Joey?* she scolded herself. *You should be grateful you have a barn-house because there your family will be together!*

Hildy brushed her tears away. Scrambling up, she turned from the river and started down the dusty country road. As she ran, she soon came to the long driveway that led to the barn-house.

Her sisters saw her coming and dashed toward her. "It's Hildy!" they cried happily. "Hildy's coming!"

Hildy staggered eagerly toward them and collapsed on the ground, eagerly hugging and kissing them all. "Oh, I love you so!" she whispered fiercely, over and over. "Every one of you!"

When Molly hurried out to greet Hildy with baby Joey on her hip, Hildy leaped up to hug them, too.

Molly looked at her curiously. "What's the matter, Hildy?" she asked.

Hildy could not answer but managed a sad smile with her tears. "Come on," she said at last. "Show me the barn-house where we all live."

She barely noticed the rotten egg smell as they all approached the part of the barn that had been converted to living quarters.

Molly seemed to realize that Hildy didn't want to talk about what had happened to Twyla's family. When the younger girls started to ask questions about it, Molly changed the subject.

As they entered the sliding door with the small window, now hung with a flour-sack curtain, Molly began leading the tour. "I'll need your father to cut a smaller door in this big one," she said. "It's too heavy to push. It locks from the inside with this big hook, but it's so hard to unlatch that I can barely do it myself."

Elizabeth spoke up then. "First, here on this wall, there's a barrel of water so we don't have to run to the tank house all the time."

Hildy glanced at the fifty-gallon drum, then on to other items stacked along the inside of the eastern barn wall. There were boxes of pots and pans, a tin-lined wood box, and a cupboard with a box set up to hold a pail of water and a wash basin.

"Now," Martha said, "we turn the corner and here's a kitchen cabinet and an old icebox underneath." She made an exaggerated gesture. "The icebox smells funny, but we don't have any ice to put in it, anyway."

Molly pointed across the room. "Our double bed will go there between the icebox and the corner—I mean, when we get a bed, it will. There'll be a dresser over there and maybe a little cupboard for clothes at the foot of the bed."

Elizabeth took over the explanations. "See the wood floor? There're so many cracks in it that it'll be easy to sweep. Just brush everything into the cracks!"

As they walked along the right wall, Martha chimed in, "The table goes here with a wood stove between it and the wall. When Molly gets a sewing machine, it'll go here, next to the clothes closet."

Sarah jumped up and down excitedly. "We'll have a couch where Ruby can sleep when she comes back," she said. "A double bed will go between it and the wall for us girls."

Hildy quickly got caught up in the spirit of the girls' enthusiasm. "Where will I sleep?" she asked.

Iola pointed to the far north wall opposite the water tank. "Right there, next to the sliding door. But if somebody forgets and opens it real fast, you'll get squished like a bug!" The little girl giggled.

Hildy laughed and grabbed Iola's hand. "What's beyond the wall they built to separate the living quarters from the rest of the barn?"

There wasn't much, the girls quickly proved. They stepped through a small door into the open part of the barn, and except for some straw on the dirt floor, the whole place was empty. High overhead, in the very center, the door was open where the Jackson fork brought in hay for storage. Pigeons fluttered nervously about, flying in and out of the high open door.

Fingers of sunlight poked through holes in the roof and knotholes in the walls. The dust the girls kicked up from walking around made them sneeze.

"Let's get out of here!" Hildy said, sneezing hard for the third time.

There were two large sliding doors on both ends of the barn section. Hildy's sisters squeezed through the nearest, the partially open northwestern door, into the barnyard. As Hildy followed, she glanced behind into the barn's soft light. A workbench and a large open storage cabinet for home-canned foods stood against the wall opposite the wood-burning stove.

"It's all beautiful!" Hildy exclaimed as they headed outside. "Beautiful!"

Elizabeth frowned. "You crazy, Hildy? It's just an ugly old barn."

Hildy dropped to her knees and quickly pulled her sister close. "Oh, don't ever say that, Elizabeth. Don't any of you ever say that. It doesn't matter what it is because we're a family, and we're all together. It doesn't matter where we live."

Elizabeth shook her head. "Does to me."

"Yeah," Martha said. "This isn't a 'forever home'!"

"I know," Hildy said, "but let's not be discouraged. I don't feel like talking right now," she added, trying to keep her voice from breaking. "But maybe I'll soon be able to tell you about something that will make you see what our family has. For now, let's go see the raccoon."

Iola yanked on the hem on Hildy's dress. "We put it in the chicken house because the trap was too small," she informed her sister.

"Yeah," Elizabeth said, brightening. "And we named it Mischief because that's what he got into the minute he was out of the box."

Hildy smiled. "What did he do?"

"What *didn't* he do?" Martha cried in mock dismay. "He knocked over the hen roosts, he tipped over the feed and water troughs, and he even tried to crawl through a little hole in the roof until we put a rock on it."

As the five sisters approached the chicken house, Hildy saw a pair of bright eyes in a masked face peering through the wire mesh over the windows. The raccoon growled as the girls paused outside the pen. The seven-foot-high sides, ends, and top were totally covered with chicken wire.

The raccoon growled again, and Iola clutched Hildy's hand. "I'm scared," she whispered.

"Mischief's scared, too," Hildy told her. "He's growling to make us think he's brave so we won't come too close."

"Uh-uh!" Iola protested. "Missy will bite me."

Elizabeth frowned. "It's Mischief, not Missy."

Iola screwed up her face. "Missy. That's the way I say it," she insisted.

Hildy reached down and swept Iola into her arms. "Mischief or Missy, it doesn't matter—except it'd better be a girl raccoon if its name is going to be Missy."

She turned back toward the house, then stopped short. A cold chill swept over her. Across the boundary fence beyond the ladino clover pasture, sat Don Gridley on his horse, watching the girls.

CHAPTER EIGHTEEN

INVITATION FROM A STRANGER

Elizabeth followed Hildy's gaze. "Who's that guy over there?" she asked.

"Don Gridley," Hildy answered. "His father's the one who didn't hold Daddy's job for him until he got back from Illinois with us."

Martha fidgeted beside Hildy. "Why's he watching us through binoculars?"

"I don't know," Hildy said honestly. "Let's ignore him. Come on. I'll race you back to the barn-house!"

The rest of the day Hildy worked hard, cleaning and helping empty the boxes they had brought from Illinois, putting their contents where they belonged.

Molly laid sleepy little Joey on a blanket in the far right corner where her bed would someday be. "Wonder what kind of neighbors we'll have," she said, returning to her work. She brushed a stray strand of hair from her smudged face.

"Friendly, I hope," Hildy replied, unwrapping a cast-iron frying pan from old newspaper. She didn't say anything about

Don Gridley, even though she knew his father must also own the adjacent land.

"Listen!" Molly said, stopping her work. "Car coming. Can't be your father this time of day."

The younger sisters rushed outside the barn-house ahead of Hildy and Molly. A pale green 1929 Model A Ford sedan putted up into the barnyard and stopped. A tall, thin woman sat behind the wheel.

Elizabeth turned to her stepmother. "Neighbor, most likely, huh?"

"Let's go find out," Molly suggested, starting toward the stranger. "'Afternoon!" she called.

"'Afternoon." The woman opened the door and stepped onto the running board. "Just moving in?" She spoke rapidly.

"Yes. I'm Molly Corrigan and these are my children." She pointed each out in turn, calling them by name.

Hildy nodded and smiled, but the other girls shyly held back. Iola hid behind Molly's skirts.

"I'm Pauline Pattman," the tall woman said, nodding to each of the children. Her words came very fast. "Me'n my husband live down the road about a mile. Maybe you've seen that chicken coop we fixed up to live in?"

Molly shook her head. Hildy didn't remember seeing the place, either.

Mrs. Pattman continued in her fast, clipped manner of speaking. "My husband's stove-up some from a bum back. I don't have nothing to bring you—hard times, you know—but I wanted to stop by and say welcome anyway."

Molly smiled. "All we want is good neighbors. Won't you come in?" she offered. "Hildy, go see if you can find the coffee pot."

As Hildy turned to obey, Mrs. Pattman raised her hand. "Sorry, folks, but I can't stay. Where'd you come from?"

"Illinois," Molly said.

Elizabeth took a step toward the woman. "But we were from

the Ozarks before that, and we've been in Texas and Missouri and lots of other places, too."

The woman laughed pleasantly. "Depression tumbleweeds, huh?"

Hildy frowned, remembering how she hated the way her father was always moving from one place to another, rootless, never caring enough to stay.

"Not anymore," Sarah spoke up. "We're going to have us a 'forever home.' "

The woman nodded. "I sure know what you mean, child. Me'n my husband are trying to make a go of it here. We're tired of being blown about by every wind of this Depression."

Molly fanned herself with her apron. "Why don't you step up against the building into the shade, Mrs. Pattman? Sorry we don't have any chairs."

"Thanks, but I don't have the time." Mrs. Pattman gave the impression of always being in a hurry. "I actually stopped by to invite you to church. You a church-going family?"

Molly hesitated a moment. "My husband isn't much for going places."

"Well, how about Sunday school for the kids?"

Hildy glanced at her stepmother, hoping she would approve. The girl felt a strong need to go to church, especially now.

Molly wiped her brow with the back of her hand. "My husband's working two jobs, seven days a week, to keep body and soul together. The kids and I have no way to get to church."

"Our church does," Mrs. Pattman said quickly. "Brother Hyde—our new preacher—bought a trailer house, and on Sunday mornings, he drives around the countryside, picking up kids and hauling them to the church in town. Brings them home afterwards, too. Can your kids come?"

Hildy glanced anxiously at her stepmother.

"I'll check with my husband," Molly said cautiously.

"Good. If he says it's okay, have them out at the end of the lane by the main road about eight-thirty Sunday morning," she said hurriedly. "Well, got to go. Nice meeting you all!"

The five Corrigan girls buzzed excitedly as the Model A putted back down the long driveway.

When their father arrived home that evening for a quick bite before going to his second job, all five girls rushed out to meet him. All except Hildy talked at once, chattering about the visitor and her invitation.

Mr. Corrigan looked down at his girls for a long moment before speaking. "What kind of a church is it?"

Hildy finally spoke. "Mrs. Pattman didn't say."

"Well," Mr. Corrigan said thoughtfully, "guess it won't hurt to let you go once."

The girls started to jump about and shout with joy.

"But," he cautioned, "that doesn't mean you can go again. Wait'll I get a report. Hildy, I'm depending on you to tell me the honest truth about what goes on at this church."

"I'll do it," Hildy answered.

"Good. Now, I've got to see your mother for a minute, then run back to the campsites. I forgot my ax."

Hildy's heart jumped. "Oh, Daddy, please let me go with you." She paused, remembering Twyla wasn't there anymore. But then another thought crossed her mind. "Maybe Spud's in town and came looking for us there."

Her father started to speak, but Hildy rushed on. "And if he's not at the campsite, maybe we could go by the post office and see if he's been there."

Joe Corrigan looked amused. "You think that boy's going to be standing around, waiting for someone to pick him up, Hildy?"

"He doesn't know where we live." Forgetting she had told the postmaster, she said, "Nobody does, except the Hocketts—if any of them are still at the bridge." She almost added that Don Gridley knew, too, but she didn't want to get into that.

Joe Corrigan took a slow breath. "I see. Well, get in the car."

As the Lexington Minuteman eased into the shallow river at the campsite, Hildy's heart filled with sadness. The Hocketts' tent still stood, but there was nobody in sight. There was only a terrible silence.

When Hildy and her father reached the eastern shore and got out of the car, Mr. Hockett's tired, sad voice called out through the tent. "Go 'way!" he cried. "We ain't got no more kids to swap!"

Tears sprang to Hildy's eyes at the awful loneliness in the man's voice. "It's us, Mr. Hockett!" she called. "Hildy Corrigan and my father."

A moment later the couple pushed the flap back on the tent. Mrs. Hockett held the baby, Kallie, in her arms.

Both parents had bloodshot eyes, and Mrs. Hockett's nose was very red from hard weeping.

"Oh!" the woman exclaimed, half-running toward Hildy and her father. "My chillern—they're all gone! Every blessed one of them 'ceptin' the baby."

"Hesh, now, woman," her husband chided softly. "It's done. Ain't no changin' that. But at least ever' one of them got a chancet to live."

Neither Hildy nor her father knew what to say. Joe Corrigan reached over and awkwardly patted Mr. Hockett on the shoulder. "Forgot my ax," he said lamely. "Can't stay. Got to get Hildy home and then get to work."

Slowly Mr. Hockett nodded. "I ain't likely to be good company now, no how. My missus, neither."

Joe Corrigan walked over to the dead tree the two men had cut down and picked up his ax. "Oh, by the way," he said, walking back toward Mr. Hockett, "has a boy about Hildy's age been around looking for her?"

Twyla's father shook his head, his eyes dull with pain. "Nobody but people wantin' to swap food fer our kids." He turned and shuffled slowly back into the tent.

Mrs. Hockett gave Hildy a long, lingering look, then followed her husband.

Hildy started to cry again. She didn't mean to. The tears just came, blurring her vision and choking her throat.

Dimly, as from a great distance, she heard her father's voice. "Come on, Hildy, let's get in the car."

Hildy thought she had cried herself out at the river hours before, but she was wrong. Fresh floods of angry, painful tears cruised down her cheeks and dropped unseen on her lap.

Her father seemed to understand her need to weep. He drove in silence to Lone River and stopped at the post office just as dusk fell.

"No sign of anybody," he said gently.

Hildy glanced around hopefully through the warm mist of her tears. She nodded. "He'll come," she said. "Maybe tomorrow. Let's go home, please."

That night, lying on a cushion of old blankets and coats, Hildy could not sleep. She lay awake long after everyone else had dozed off. The first night in the barn-house was strange. She heard high-pitched squeaking sounds and knew that bats were flying around inside the barn. Hildy tried not to think about them. And she also tried not to think about Twyla. It hurt too much. But Twyla had become a part of Hildy she would never forget.

Hildy turned her thoughts to Spud. *Where is he?* she wondered. *He should have reached Lone River by now.*

Then her thoughts jumped to Ruby. *Had she found any clue to her father's whereabouts in Grizzly Gulch?* Soon Ruby would return and Hildy would find out.

The vision of Don Gridley watching them from across the pasture burned in Hildy's mind. She tried to shake off the uneasy feeling his unexpected presence had given her, but she couldn't.

Hildy turned over on her back and laced her fingers behind her hair, now loose and untidy. She stared at the dark ceiling. *Oh, Lord,* she prayed, *I'm so mixed up. I'm glad for the barn-house. It's better than the tent. And I'm glad we're going to church. But I'm hurt and mad, too.*

She poured out her anguish in a long, silent prayer. For a long time the hurt, anger, and frustration spilled out. Somehow, just telling God how she felt seemed to help. Finally, spent in both body and mind, Hildy whispered her *amen* aloud and slept.

Sunday morning each of the five Corrigan sisters was dressed in her only good dress and shoes. As they waited in the shade of the Lombardy poplars at the end of the lane, Hildy felt empty, drained, like an old discarded eggshell.

Soon a black Chevrolet sedan pulling a trailer house pulled up beside the girls and stopped. The driver, a nice-looking man with a gentle face and glasses, leaned out of the window. "I'm Brother Hyde," he announced. "You must be the Corrigan children Mrs. Pattman told me about."

Hildy nodded, instantly liking the man in a dark hat and blue serge suit. She introduced herself and her sisters.

The preacher repeated each girl's name, then got out of the car and led them to the trailer house.

As they followed, Hildy noticed that Brother Hyde's pants were very shiny, showing wear. So was the back of his suit. The cuffs of his pants were frayed above the run-down heels of his shoes. Preaching didn't pay well in Lone River, Hildy decided.

Brother Hyde opened the door to the trailer house. "I'm sorry your parents couldn't join us," he commented. "Maybe another time."

Inside, the trailer house was crowded with kids from toddlers to teens. "These are the Corrigan kids," the preacher said as Hildy and her sisters climbed in. "You others introduce yourselves."

Hildy and her sisters enjoyed the bumpy, raucous ride into town with all the other kids. Hildy had seen many homemade trailers before, but this one was different. It was factory made, about twelve feet long, and there were kids crammed into every little space.

Finally the trailer stopped in front of a glistening white stucco church. It was a simple, box-like structure with a short, square bell tower in front.

The pastor came back and opened the trailer door. "We're here," he announced. "Some of you boys and girls who've been here before please show the Corrigan children where their class-rooms will be. I'll park the trailer and see you all later."

As Hildy and her sisters followed their guides up the steep concrete steps, a dog barked sharply behind them. Hildy didn't pay any attention until a voice called from the street.

"Hildy?"

She grabbed the handrail and spun around in surprise. "Spud!" she cried. "And Lindy!"

Hildy pushed her way past her sisters and down the stairs toward the grinning boy and his tan and black dog on the side-walk.

CHAPTER NINETEEN

SPUD CLASHES WITH DON GRIDLEY

At the bottom of the steep church stairs, Hildy paused two feet in front of Spud.

He grinned at her, his green eyes sparkling. "Hi," he said, absently patting Lindy's head.

The dog whined and thrust his brown muzzle into Hildy's hand. "Hi," she replied. Her voice sounded funny, a little squeaky and excited.

In some ways, Spud looked the same as when she had last seen him in Oklahoma. Although two years older than Hildy, he was about her height, strongly built with wide shoulders, a narrow waist, and hands too big for his body. He had a ruddy complexion with lots of freckles and a wide, friendly grin.

"Hi," Spud said again. "Lindy's glad to see you." He paused, then added, "Me, too."

Hildy was smiling so hard her cheeks hurt. There was an awkward silence. She looked down at Lindy and rubbed his ears. Lindy was an Airedale with short, wiry, black and tan hair.

His tail had been cut off about six inches from his sturdy body. As Hildy stroked the collarless dog, she thought about how he'd gotten his name. Spud had said he'd named the Airedale after the famous aviator, Charles Lindbergh, who had astounded the world a few years earlier by flying the Atlantic Ocean alone in a single engine airplane.

Hildy looked up and had an urge to reach out and touch Spud. Instead, she sized him up and down and said, "I like your cowboy clothes."

The first time she saw him in the Ozarks, Spud had worn knickers to just below the knees, and he had tied the loose sole of one of his shoes on with a piece of string to keep it from flopping. Now his working cowboy's outfit looked perfect, except for the aviator-type cap he always wore in honor of Lindbergh, his hero.

Spud looked down at the faded blue jeans, matching shirt, and scuffed cowboy boots. "These are the same ones your Uncle Cecil gave me before you left," he replied. "His boss's wife just cut them down and took them in a little to fit better."

Hildy giggled. "You once called Uncle Cecil a 'diminutive troglodyte'! Remember?"

"I remember. Say, you still got my dictionary?"

"Sure have. I learn a new word almost every day. Hey, when did you get in, anyway?"

"Just this morning. I started asking around, but nobody seemed to know where you lived."

"I've been watching for you at the post office," Hildy assured him. "My father and I stopped by to look just the other night."

"Well, you can stop looking."

She smiled. "Where's your bindle?" she asked, referring to the short stick with a large blue and white polka dot handkerchief in which Spud used to carry his few worldly possessions.

"Graduated to a suitcase," he replied. "Left it at the stage depot until I could find you." He glanced up at the church and the steps where Hildy's four sisters stared at him. "You go to this church?"

"Never saw it before." She briefly told him how she and her sisters happened to be here. "Come on up and meet my sisters, then go to Sunday school with us," she urged.

He hesitated. "These aren't proper clothes. Besides, it's been a long time since I was in a church, Hildy."

"Forget the clothes. And this is a good time to start going again." She reached out and grabbed his hand. "Come on."

"In a minute." The boy released her fingers and led the dog to a small patch of lawn in front of the church. "Stay, Lindy, stay."

Spud then followed Hildy up the stairs. "Where's your pugnacious tomboy cousin?" he asked.

"Ruby's in Grizzly Gulch, looking for her father. I'll tell you all about that later." Hildy turned to her sisters and introduced them to Spud.

They all held back, shy and silent, except for little Iola. "Are you Hildy's boyfriend?" she asked innocently.

"Iola!" Hildy scolded in embarrassment. "Don't say things like that. Come on, everybody. Let's go inside."

Hildy's face felt warm, and she didn't look at Spud as they all entered the church together. They were quickly surrounded by adults and other young people who greeted the newcomers warmly.

Everyone wore old but clean clothes. Hard times had obviously hit these parishioners, too. Hildy guessed that most of the men were farmers or laborers like her father. When she shook hands, whether with a man or a woman, Hildy noticed the hard, work-calloused palms. She knew that her own hands must have felt the same to others.

Everyone separated for Sunday school except Hildy and Spud. Their age group met in a musty-smelling basement. Hildy's mind was in such turmoil—excitement over seeing Spud, yet hurt over Twyla's situation—that she heard little of the lesson. However, after the class, she found the church service very interesting.

Hildy guessed that fifty to seventy-five people were seated

in the small church building. The large windows had colored paper pasted over the panes to resemble stained glass. The pews were old with three-inch-thick cushions. A long, slightly curved altar stretched across the front of the first row of pews, and there was a raised choir loft and pulpit behind the altar.

During the service, the people knelt in the pews for prayer. Hildy felt a little awkward as she and Spud did the same. But as the prayers began, Hildy's mind turned to Twyla and her family. She prayed silently for them, feeling a dull ache inside.

Then the prayer time ended, and Brother Hyde stepped to the pulpit. "Please turn with me in your Bibles to the third chapter of Proverbs, verses five and six."

Hildy hadn't thought to bring her Bible, and there were none in the pew rack in front of her. She listened as the pastor read aloud the first few words from the familiar King James Version. " 'Trust in the Lord with all thine heart; and lean not unto thine own understanding. . . .' "

There it is again! she thought. *That verse my grandmother quoted, the one I memorized and remembered just when I needed it down by the river!*

She raised her eyes, wondering if this was the answer she had needed about Twyla and the Hockett family's awful troubles.

She glanced at Spud. He was gazing up at the preacher and didn't seem to notice her.

Hildy barely heard the rest of the sermon as those few simple words from Proverbs rang reassuringly through her mind.

The preacher ended the service by inviting everyone to stand and sing "Just As I Am." When the people began to sing the hymn, Brother Hyde raised his voice. "Whatever your needs, the altar is open for prayer."

Hildy stirred. She wanted to go forward and kneel there. She had done that years before in the little Ozark church she had attended with her mother. But after her mother's death, Hildy had closed her heart to God, only learning to trust Him again recently. The experiences of the last several days had certainly tested her.

Hildy decided not to go down front to the altar. She didn't want to leave Spud alone. Besides, she already felt better. She knew now that she didn't have to understand all the terrible happenings of the week. She could trust the Lord to work them out. Hildy took a deep breath and looked again at Spud.

He hadn't been to church in many years, he had said. He was not singing the hymn but looking down at the floor. Hildy wondered what he was thinking.

After church, Hildy found her sisters outside and warned them to stay close so they could get a ride home in the pastor's trailer house. Brother Hyde had told them he would be a while because he had to shake hands with everybody first.

Hildy and Spud walked over to the church's small patch of lawn and sat under a sycamore tree with Lindy. The dog nearly twisted himself in half, showing his affection for Hildy as well as his master.

"You look different, somehow, Spud," Hildy said, petting Lindy's head.

"How so?"

"Maybe a little taller?"

"The boots," he explained, sticking out the one on his right foot. "But my mother told me my brothers started growing like crazy when they were about my age, so maybe I'm starting, too."

Hildy stirred uneasily, her hand resting on Lindy's head. "Did you ever make up with your folks?"

"Yes and no. I thought I hated my old man for always knocking me around. But Mrs. Witt—remember her?"

"Of course. The wife of Uncle Cecil's boss in Oklahoma. How is she?"

"She's fine. Said to say hello. Anyway, while I was working on the ranch, she kept after me to make things right with my folks."

"So did you?"

"I wrote them and let them know where I was and where I was planning to go."

Hildy reached out impulsively and touched the boy's freck-led hand. "I'm glad. How long had it been?"

"About three years."

"I imagine they were very glad to hear from you after all that time."

"Maybe so. I haven't heard back yet."

Hildy thoughtfully considered Spud. He, like Hildy, was strong-willed, even stubborn. Yet he was a runaway, and that bothered Hildy, since family was so important to her. "How long can you stay?" she asked.

He shrugged. "I don't know."

Suddenly a voice called mockingly from the nearby sidewalk. "Well, now, if it isn't the hillbilly gal from the Ozarks! Come to see the big city, did you?"

Hildy spun around in surprise to see Don Gridley standing astride his bicycle, both feet resting on the concrete sidewalk.

Spud nudged Hildy. "Who's that?" he asked quietly.

"Don Gridley," Hildy replied. "His father owns most of this county."

"He called you a hillbilly. Why?"

"Oh, it's nothing. Ruby and I just got on his bad side, that's all."

Don called again. "Is your boyfriend a hillbilly, too?"

Instantly, Spud's quick temper flared. He leaped to his feet, and Lindy jumped up, too, growling. Hildy threw her arms around the dog's neck and held him.

"I'm not a hillbilly!" Spud snapped.

"Yeah?" Don sneered. "Then how come you're hanging around with one?"

Spud strode across the lawn in a few quick steps. His voice was low and hard as he thrust his face within inches of the other boy's. "Don't you ever call Hildy that—or any other derogatory name! You understand?"

Hildy felt Lindy's hackles rise. "No, Lindy," she whispered. "Stay." She released her grip as the dog sat on his haunches.

Hildy walked over to where the two boys were glowering at each other.

"And if I don't?" Don challenged.

"You don't want to find out," Spud said evenly.

Hildy tugged on Spud's arm. "Please don't."

Spud took a slow, deep breath, then nodded, his eyes still locked on the other boy's face. "Don, or whatever your name is, remember what I said." He backed up slowly with Hildy close beside him.

Don straightened his bicycle and started pedaling rapidly down the sidewalk. When he was about fifty feet away, he turned and waved his fist. "You'll both be sorry!" he yelled.

A shiver passed over Hildy's shoulders. She tried to smile reassuringly at Spud, but it failed. Instead, she said, "Thanks, but I think you've made an enemy, and it's my fault."

"I can take care of myself," Spud assured her. "Been doing it for a long time, hoboing."

Hildy changed the subject, although her unspoken fear of Don Gridley remained. "Let's go ask Brother Hyde if he'll let you ride in the trailer house," she suggested. "I want my folks to meet you."

"What about Lindy? Can he ride along?"

"Let's ask the pastor."

Brother Hyde asked Hildy and Spud several questions, then agreed. "If you're sure your folks won't mind your bringing home a guest like this, Hildy."

On the drive into the country, Hildy told Spud about Twyla. Hildy's eyes were moist as she concluded, "I guess I'll never understand it, but the preacher's Bible verse is helping me to live with what happened."

Spud sighed. "I don't know what to say, except I'm sorry," he said softly.

About one-thirty, as the Corrigan kids, Spud, and Lindy got out of the trailer house, Elizabeth pointed up the lane toward the barn-house. "Look!" she cried. "Ruby's back!"

Hildy glanced up to see her cousin waving. Ruby was smiling, her short-cut blond hair reflecting the sunlight. Hildy waved back in greeting.

Spud looked confused. "I thought you said she was up in Grizzly Gulch."

Hildy nodded. "She was. I wonder if she found her father. Come on. Let's find out."

They all ran toward Ruby, who was also running to meet them. Hildy suddenly remembered how Spud and Ruby always got into arguments. She looked imploringly at Spud. "Please try to get along with her, okay?"

"Okay."

Hildy flashed a thankful smile and turned to hug her cousin. "Ruby! Did you find your father?"

Her cousin looked straight at Spud, her eyes bright with challenge. "Nope," she answered. "Not yet, but I got me a plumb good idee where he's at."

Spud stepped forward a little. "Hello, Ruby," he said.

"Howdy," she replied.

Hildy heaved a big sigh of relief. "Hey, that's great, Ruby! Tell us all about it."

As they all continued up the lane to the barn-house, Ruby told them about her search in the Mother Lode ghost town of Grizzly Gulch. "I asked purt' near ever'body there if'n they'd heerd of a man called 'Highpockets' Konning. Nobody had until yestiddy."

"What happened?" Hildy asked excitedly.

Ruby explained. "Jist about the time I thunk I wasn't never goin' to find hide ner hair o' him, I met this here ol' lady who had an address fer 'im. She give it to me jist afore the woman where I worked brung me home. I'm gonna write tomorry!"

Hildy grinned. "You'll find him, Ruby. I know you will."

After Spud was introduced to Hildy's stepmother, they all had a lunch of biscuits, which had been baked in the wood-burning stove, and "greens," or wild weeds. Molly had gathered them that morning and cooked them. They looked and tasted like spinach. It wasn't very tasty, but it was all the family had to eat.

After lunch the smaller kids rested on their pallets while Hildy, Elizabeth, and Martha showed Ruby and Spud around the ranch.

By the time they came to the far boundary fence, Hildy was pleased that Spud and Ruby seemed to be getting along. They turned around and started back.

Suddenly Elizabeth pointed. "Hey! There's that kid who keeps watching us."

Hildy looked up in time to see Don Gridley spurring his horse rapidly away from the barn-house.

In fear, Hildy glanced that way, then screamed. "Fire! The barn-house is on fire!"

CHAPTER
TWENTY

FIRE! FIRE!

Hildy ran frantically toward the barn-house. Yellow flames leaped up at the far end of the old, dry, wooden structure. Thick black smoke boiled into the summer sky.

Oh, Lord, help! Hildy prayed. "Molly!" she screamed. "Fire! The place is on fire!"

Although Hildy was running with all her might, Ruby and Spud outran her as well as Elizabeth and Martha. Hildy's desperate eyes searched for signs of her stepmother, two little sisters, and baby Joey.

"They're probably all taking naps!" she called through ragged gasps for air.

Spud reached the sliding door at the corner of the living quarters and tried to slide it open. It wouldn't move.

Hildy remembered Molly's earlier complaint about the inside latch. "It works hard!" she yelled.

Spud pounded on the door with the palm of his hand and kicked with his boots. "Mrs. Corrigan! Fire! The barn's on fire and I can't get the door open!"

Almost to the barn, Hildy gasped for breath. Her heart was

beating so fast it seemed about to burst. "Run around to the other side!" she yelled to Spud. "Hurry!"

While he raced around to the near east side, Ruby dashed along the north wall toward the western sliding door. Lindy barked excitedly and bounded after his master.

Hildy, Elizabeth, and Martha headed straight for the sliding door that wouldn't open. There a small, frightened face appeared at the small glass window in the door.

Hildy gasped. "Sarah!" she yelled. "Unhook the latch, fast!"

"I can't!" came the frightened words through the barn door. The towheaded girl frantically slapped her open palm against the window.

"Don't!" Hildy yelled. "You'll cut yourself. I'll get you out."

Reaching the barn, Hildy threw her weight against the heavy sliding door. It didn't budge.

She turned to the small window and waved her ashen-faced little sister away. "Stand back! I'm going to break the glass!"

Sarah disappeared from the window as Hildy turned to look for something to use. In all the confusion of the others' yelling, practical Elizabeth had turned on the garden hose at the corner faucet and was trying to squirt the stream upward toward the fire.

"Molly!" Hildy yelled. "Molly! Can you hear me?"

There was no answer. Hildy picked up the first thing she saw—the empty box trap. Running toward the window, she slammed the box trap through the glass. It exploded in flying shards. Instantly, Hildy shifted the box and ran it around the edges, knocking out small pieces of glass that hadn't fallen in.

Hildy stuck her head inside and squinted to see in the semi-dark room. "Molly! Molly! Where are you?"

A slight groan came from a short distance away. Hildy's eyes flickered toward the sound. "Molly, get up! The house is on fire!"

"I . . . can't." Molly's voice was weak. "I fell and hit my head, and I think my leg's broken, too."

"We'll get you out," Hildy promised. "Where's Iola and

Joey?" Hildy tried to crawl through the window, but tiny pieces of broken glass cut her hands. She jerked them back, realizing the window was too high and too small.

Molly called to her weakly. "I've got the baby, Hildy. Iola was here a moment ago . . . Iola, where are you?" Molly's voice rose to a scream.

Hildy remembered what her youngest sister had said once about what she'd do in a fire. "I'd hide in a closet!"

There was no closet in the barn, but Hildy was sure Iola had hidden somewhere in the huge, old building.

Hildy turned, fright drying her mouth. "Elizabeth, run around and tell Spud and Ruby that Iola's missing," she ordered. "Martha, help me find Daddy's ax."

"It's right there by the woodpile!" Martha replied in a near screech.

"Get it for me, but don't cut yourself." Hildy spun around to stick her head back through the broken window. "Molly, can you crawl?"

"I'm . . . trying. But holding the baby—" Molly's voice broke off.

"Keep trying!" Hildy yelled. "See if you can unlatch the door. I can't reach it." She turned back to her sister outside. "Martha, pull a box or something up to here, and I'll help you climb through the window."

Then she vaguely heard Ruby and Spud shouting and realized they had found a way into the main part of the barn, but they were not yet in the living quarters.

Martha stood behind Hildy, gasping for air. "Here's the ax."

Hildy turned and grabbed it. She took a quick step back and braced herself to swing at the barn door. Then she heard sirens. Holding the ax above her head, she glanced down the lane. An old Liberty fire engine turned off the main road followed by a stream of volunteers in old cars.

"Thank God," Hildy breathed. "Somebody must have seen the smoke and called the fire department."

Spud's voice came from inside the barn door. "The back

door's open. I'm going in after them."

Hildy lowered the ax. "I'll be able to help you if you come and lift the latch once you get inside!" she yelled.

A moment later, she heard the metal hook lift. On the count of three, she and Spud pulled on the heavy door from each side. It slid open.

Sarah darted into the open, screaming with fright. Elizabeth quickly dropped the garden hose and grabbed Sarah by the hand.

"Get back, both of you!" Hildy yelled. "You, too, Martha!"

Hildy jumped through the open door into the living quarters. Dense smoke curled down from the roof, choking Hildy. She heard an echoing cough and saw Spud trying to help Molly along the floor. Ruby had scooped up the screaming baby Joey and rushed him toward the door.

"Iola!" Hildy cried. "She's gone! She's probably hiding from the flames. I'll find her."

"Wait!" Spud yelled as he pulled Molly through the open door. "Let the firemen do that."

"I can't wait!" Hildy plunged into the smoke-filled room and stumbled over an empty box. She fell hard, scratching her shins, but she didn't stop.

There was less smoke close to the wooden floor, and Hildy could breathe better. Sobbing with fear, her heart pounding, Hildy crawled across the room on her hands and knees. "Iola!" she called, still choking from the smoke. "Where are you?"

"Hiding from the fire!" The tiny, scared voice came from somewhere in the smoky room.

"Don't hide. Come to me."

"I'm too scared!"

Hildy crawled rapidly toward the voice. "Keep talking, Iola. I'll find you. You hear me?"

"Ye-e-es." The voice seemed fainter.

"Oh, Lord," Hildy's voice cracked in spontaneous prayer, "help me find her fast." She called to her little sister again. "Iola, can you see me?"

"Ye-e-es."

"Keep talking." Hildy choked on the smoke. "Call my name. Just keep saying it over and over so I can hear you: Hildy, Hildy, Hildy."

Like a tiny echo, the answer came. "Hildy . . . Hildy . . ."

Hearing the flames crackling along the tinder-dry shingles, Hildy crawled quickly along the floor, ignoring the splinters tearing her arms and knees.

"Here I am, Hildy." The voice was to the right.

Hildy swung around, barely able to see her little sister through the smoke. "Thank God!" Hildy cried, reaching out and yanking Iola from an empty wooden crate.

As Hildy turned, she heard Spud's voice right behind her. "I'll take her. Here, grab my other hand and we'll be out of here in no time!"

At the door the fire chief and his volunteers met them, and Hildy breathed deeply of the fresh air. In moments, the survivors huddled tightly in relief while the firemen and neighbors doused the flames.

The tanker's big hoses quickly controlled the fire. Other cars arrived, bringing neighbors with offers of help, and encouraging, welcoming words.

The fire chief, a local grocery store owner still wearing his green apron, came up to Molly where she huddled with the children. He removed his hat. "The far west side's pretty well gone," he reported, "but there's no real damage to the living quarters on the east except for the smoke. Good thing one of your neighbors had a phone and called in the alarm so fast."

Just then Mrs. Pattman rushed up, interrupting. "Let me see about your head, Mrs. Corrigan. Looks like a cut. And let's see that leg, too!"

Molly started to protest, but the tall, fast-talking neighbor woman was already checking over the injuries. "That scalp cut'll heal without stitches," she announced. "And I think your leg's just twisted."

Hildy watched the fire chief reach into his apron pocket as Mrs. Pattman stepped back.

Molly smiled up at her well-meaning neighbor. "Thank you, Mrs. Pattman. Would you mind taking the children over there out of the way for a minute? I want to talk to the chief. Hildy, you, Spud, and Ruby, please stay."

Hildy pushed closer with Spud and Ruby, trying to see what the fire chief had in his hands. "You folks ever see this before?" he asked.

They all shook their heads.

The chief nodded. "That's what I thought," he said. "It's an ordinary mousetrap, which was used to set the fire. See how it works?" He held it up to demonstrate. "Kitchen matches are placed here on the trigger. The trap is set, held open with tape. Then when the sun melts the 'stickum,' the tape lets go and releases the metal bar. It strikes the matches and they flare up."

He pointed. "We found this over there in the dry grass against the western side of the barn."

Hildy gasped. "Daddy said he'd have to cut those weeds as soon as he could."

"Well," the chief went on, "somebody apparently set a couple of these traps, starting the fire. This one didn't go off. So we have the evidence. It's definitely arson."

Molly's hand flew to her mouth. "You mean—?"

"Sure do. You got any idea who'd want to burn you out?"

Molly shook her head.

Hildy hesitated, thinking about Don Gridley's threats and seeing him ride away. She suddenly remembered that she had never apologized for falsely accusing him of stealing her father's watch. She would have to do that later. Meantime, she didn't want to falsely accuse him of arson.

Ruby didn't hesitate. "We seen that thar Don Gridley a-ridin' away like the wind jist afore we seen the smoke," she said. "He done it!"

Spud leaned over to the fire chief. "He did threaten Hildy and me in town today."

The fire chief nodded. "I'm not surprised. That boy's been in trouble about fires before. Some claimed he burned down the original ranch house here, but there was no proof. However, if it turns out he did set this one . . ."

As the chief left his sentence unfinished, Hildy asked, "Then what'll happen to him?"

"Well, the last time this happened, his father promised me that he'd get medical help for the boy if he did it again. My guess is that Don Gridley will be going away for a while."

Hildy was relieved, but all she said was, "Thanks for saving our house. And thanks to you, Spud and Ruby!" she rushed on, smiling at them.

"You're the one who saved the little girl," Spud reminded her.

"She's my sister," Hildy said softly. "And we're a family."

Ruby hugged her cousin. "We're all family," she added.

That night, after Joe Corrigan got home, the family stood with Spud and Ruby outside the barn-house, looking at the partially burned building. For a while, everyone just stood there silently.

Then Hildy spoke up. "It's strange how it all turned out. I mean, all those people we'd never met offering us food and fresh milk each day for the kids, and all that."

Ruby swallowed noticeably. "That one woman said she'd give me board and room if I'd help with the housework."

Spud nodded. "And Mrs. Pattman wants me to help around her place until her husband's feeling better."

Joe Corrigan hugged his wife. "I can't get over the way the men said they'd help repair the barn and fix up the living quarters. We got us some real nice neighbors."

There was silence again; then he added, "I drove over the bridge today. The Hocketts' tent is gone. There's nothing there except some trampled grass and ashes where the fire pits were."

Hildy choked back a sob just as a chirring sound from the chicken pen caused everyone to look around.

Hildy smiled in spite of her painful memories. "Mischief seems lonesome," she remarked. "I think that's one raccoon that'll make a good pet real soon."

Everyone chuckled; then Hildy's father cleared his throat. "Let's all join hands," he said, taking Molly's in his right and Hildy's in his left.

Puzzled, Hildy reached out and took Spud's hand, and he, in turn, reached for Ruby's. In seconds, they had all joined hands in a circle.

Hildy watched her father as he looked slowly from one face to another. Then he bowed his head. "Lord . . ." he said so softly that Hildy barely heard, "Lord, you know I don't know how to talk to you anymore, and I don't know what to say. But you know what I'm thinking. Thanks."

Hildy looked up in the dimming light of dusk. It had only been about three weeks since they left Illinois, yet so many things had happened.

Hildy still didn't understand much of it. She didn't know why her father had suddenly uttered a short prayer, and she certainly didn't understand why such a terrible thing had happened to Twyla and her family. Hildy ached just thinking about her friend whom she would never see again.

Yet, through it all, Hildy had learned some things. Again the words echoed through her mind, *"Trust in the Lord . . . and lean not to thine own understanding. . . ."*

Hildy also knew that in spite of the Depression, she and her family, as well as Spud and Ruby, would make it—somehow. They had no worldly goods of value, but they were a family— a family together with friends—and that was what really mattered.

Aloud, Hildy said, "As for our 'forever home,' it isn't the building or place that counts, but the family being together."

Little Sarah tugged Hildy's arm. "But we'll still find that 'forever home' someday, won't we?"

Hildy nodded. "Sure we will." She glanced at her family, then at Spud and Ruby. "And Ruby will find her father, and Spud . . . well, he'll find what's right for him, too."

"Oh, boy!" Sarah exclaimed. "I can hardly wait to see how it all works out."

"Me, too," Hildy said sincerely. "Me, too."